F. Anstey

Tourmalin's Time Cheques

F. Anstey

Tourmalin's Time Cheques

ISBN/EAN: 9783337193027

Printed in Europe, USA, Canada, Australia, Japan

Cover: Foto ©Andreas Hilbeck / pixelio.de

More available books at **www.hansebooks.com**

TOURMALIN'S TIME CHEQUES

BY

F. ANSTEY

AUTHOR OF VICE VERSÂ, THE TINTED VENUS,
THE BLACK POODLE, ETC.

NEW YORK
D. APPLETON AND COMPANY
1891

CONTENTS.

PROLOGUE.

CHAPTER I.

TOURMALIN'S FIRST CHEQUE AND HOW HE TOOK IT.

CHAPTER II.

THE SECOND CHEQUE.

CHAPTER VII.

THE CULMINATING CHEQUE.

CHAPTER VIII.

PAID IN HIS OWN COIN.

CHAPTER IX.

COMPOUND INTEREST.

CHAPTER X.

TOURMALIN'S TIME CHEQUES.

THE PROLOGUE.

*On Deck.—Curry and Culture.—Alternative Distractions.
—A Period of Probation.—The Oath and the Talis-
man.—Wavering.—A Chronological Error.—The Time
Bargain.—Tourmalin Opens an Account.*

MR. PETER TOURMALIN was sitting, or rather
lying, in a steamer-chair, on the first-class saloon-deck of the P. and O. ship *Boomerang*,
which had not been many days as yet on the
voyage home from Sydney. He had been
trying to read; but it was a hot morning, and
the curry, of which he had partaken freely
at breakfast, had made him feel a little heavy
and disinclined for mental exertion just then,
particularly as Buckle's *History of Civilization*, the first volume of which he had brought

up from the ship's library, is not exactly light literature at any time.

He wanted distraction of some sort, but he could not summon up sufficient energy to rise and pace the deck, as his only acquaintance on board, a Mr. Perkins, was doing with a breezy vigor which Tourmalin found himself feebly resenting.

Another alternative was open to him, it is true: not far away were other deck-chairs, in which some of the lady passengers were reading, writing, and chatting more or less languidly. There were not very many on board —for it was autumn, a time at which home-wardbound vessels are not apt to be crowded —but even in that small group there were one or two with whom it might have seemed possible to pass a little time in a pleasant and profitable manner. For instance, there was that tall, graceful girl in the navy-blue skirt, and the striped cotton blouse confined at her slender waist by a leathern belt. (Tourmalin, it should be mentioned, was in the habit of noticing the details of feminine costume.) She had regular features, gray eyes which lighted up whenever she spoke, and an expression of singular nobility and sweetness; her fair hair was fastened up in loose gleaming masses under her highly becoming straw hat.

Peter watched her surreptitiously, from time to time, from behind the third page of Buckle. She was attempting to read a novel; but her attention, like his own, wandered occasionally, and he even fancied that he surprised her now and then in the act of glancing at himself with a certain interest.

Near her was another girl, not quite so tall, and darker, but scarcely less pleasing in appearance. She wore a cool-looking pink frock, and her luxuriant bronze tresses were set off by a simple white flannel cap. She held some embroidery in her listless fingers, but was principally occupied in gazing out to sea with a wistful and almost melancholy expression. Her eyes were soft and brown, and her features piquantly irregular; giving Peter, who considered himself no mean judge of female character, the impression of a highly emotional and enthusiastic temperament. He thought he saw signs that she also honored him by her notice.

Peter was a flat-headed little man, with

weak eyes and flaxen hair; but even flat-
headed little men may indulge these fancies
at times, without grossly deceiving themselves.
He knew, as one does learn such things on
board ship, that the name of the first young
lady was Tyrrell, and that she was the daughter of a judge who had been spending the
Long Vacation in a voyage to recruit his
health. Of the other, he knew no more than
that she was a Miss Davenport.

At present, however, he had no personal
acquaintance with either of them, and, in fact,
as has already been said, knew nobody on
board to speak to, except the energetic Mr.
Perkins, a cheery man with a large fund of
general information, who was going home on
some business connected with a banking house
in Melbourne.

And yet it is not difficult to make acquaint-
ances on board ship, if a man cares to do so;
accident or design will provide opportunities
in plenty, and two or three days at sea are
equivalent to at least as many weeks on shore.
And Peter being quite aware of these facts,
and by no means indifferent to the society of
the other sex, which, indeed he considered

more 'interesting than that of his own, it
would seem that he must have had some strong
reason for having kept studiously apart from
the social life on board the *Boomerang*.

He had a reason, and it was this: he was
an engaged man, and on his probation. A
bachelor, still under thirty, of desultory hab-
its which unfitted him to shine in any pro-
fession, he had a competency—that refuge of
the incompetent—which made him independ-
ent.

Some months previously he had had the
good fortune to meet with a lady somewhat
his junior in years, but endowed with charms
of mind and character which excited his ad-
miration and reverence. He recognized that
she supplied the qualities in which he felt himself deficient; he was weary of the rather
purposeless life he had led. He wanted a wife
who would regulate and organize his existence; and Miss Sophia Pinceney, with her
decision and her thoroughness, was eminently
the person to do it. So it was not long before he took courage and proposed to her.

Miss Pinceney, though she had been highly
educated, and possessed a considerable fortune

of her own, was by no means inclined to look
unfavorably upon such a suitor. He might not
be quite her intellectual equal, but he was anxious to improve his mind. He was amiable
and amenable, and altogether likely, under careful guidance, to prove an excellent husband.

But she was prudent, and reason told her
that the suddenness of Peter's passion was no
guarantee of its enduring qualities. She had
heard and seen too much of a rather catholic
susceptibility in his nature, to feel it safe to incur so grave a risk as marriage until she had
certain proof that his attachment to her was
robust enough to bear the severest test; and
to that test she was determined to submit him.

She consented to an engagement on one
condition, that he was to take a long voyage.
If he returned in the same mind, she would
be sufficiently sure of his constancy to marry
him as soon as he wished : if he did not, her
misgivings would be amply justified. There
was very little sentiment about Sophia; she
took a practical and philosophical view of
the marriage union, as became a disciple of
Ibsen.

"I like you, Peter," she told him frankly;

"you have many qualities that endear you to me, but I don't feel that I can depend upon you at present. And from what I know of you, I fear it is only too probable that absence and the attractive society of a passenger-ship may lead you to discover that you have mistaken the depth of the feeling you entertain for me."

"But look here, Sophia," he had expostulated; "if you're afraid of that, why do you make me go?"

"Because," she had replied, with her admirable common sense, "because, if my fears should prove to be unhappily only too well-founded, I shall, at least, have made the discovery before it is too late."

And, in spite of all his protests, Peter had to go. Sophia sought to reconcile him to this necessity by pointing out the advantages of travel, the enlarging effect it would have upon his mind, and the opportunities a long sea-voyage afforded for regular and uninterrupted study on the lines she had already mapped out for him; but despite these consolations, he went away in low spirits. When the moment came for parting, even the strong-minded Sophia was seized with a kind of compunction.

"Something tells me, Peter," she said, " that the ordeal will prove too much for you: in spite of your good resolutions, you will sooner or later be drawn into some flirtation which will make you forget me. I know you so well, Peter!"

"I wish you could show a little more confidence in me," he had answered in a wounded tone. "Since I met you, Sophia, I have ceased to be the butterfly I was. But as you seem to doubt me, it may relieve your mind if I promise faithfully that, while I am away from you, I will never, under any inducement, allow myself to overstep the limits of the most ordinary civility toward any woman with whom I may be brought in contact. I swear it, Sophia! Are you satisfied now?"

Perhaps he had a secret prevision that a time might come when this oath would prove a salutary restraint upon his straying fancy, and it certainly had an immediate and most reassuring effect upon Sophia.

Tourmalin had gone out to Australia, had seen something of the country during his stay in the colony, and was now, as we have seen, on his return ; and during the whole time his oath, to his great credit, had been literally and faithfully kept.

During the voyage out, he had been too persistently unwell to be inclined to dally with sentiment; but in his subsequent wanderings, he had avoided, or rather escaped, all intercourse with any Colonial ladies who might by any possibility affect his allegiance to Sophia, whose image consequently still held undisputed possession of his heart.

In case he should feel himself wavering at any time, he had been careful to provide himself with a talisman in the shape of a photograph, the mere sight of which would be instantly effectual. But somehow, since he had been on board the *Boomerang*, the occasions on which he had been driven to refer to this photograph had been growing more and more frequent; while, at the same time, he had a tormenting consciousness that it took an increasingly longer time to work.

He brought it out now, and studied it attentively. It was the likeness of a girl without any great pretensions to beauty, with dark hair rolled neatly back from a massive brow that shone with intellectuality; penetrating eyes, whose keenness was generally tempered by folding glasses; a large, firm mouth, and a square chin; altogether, the face of a young woman who would stand no trifling.

He put it back respectfully in his pocket; but the impulse to go across and drop, in an accidental fashion, into a vacant seat near one of those two girls was still unconquered. He was feeling so dull; he had got such a very little way into the *History of Civilization*, a work which he was reading rather for Sophia's satisfaction than his own, and there was such a lot more of it! Might he not allow himself a brief holiday, and beguile the long weary morning with a little cheerful conversation? It was most unlikely, strict etiquette being by general consent suspended on board ship, that either young lady would resent a hazarded remark—at all events, he could but try.

But then his oath—his rash and voluntary oath to Sophia—what of that? He had not, it was true, debarred himself from ordinary civility; but could he be sure of keeping always within those bounds if the acquaintanceship was once established? He had reasons for doubting this very seriously. And, besides, had not Sophia more than hinted in her last letter that, as a reward for his fidelity, she might join the ship at Gibraltar with her mother, and so put an earlier end to his term of probation? He could not be too careful. After holding out so long, it would be madness to relax his precautions now. No, he would resist these Sirens, like a modern Ulysses; though, in the latter's case, the Sirens were not actually on board, and, even then, the hero had to be lashed to the mast. But Tourmalin felt confident, notwithstanding, that he would prove at least as obdurate as the wily Greek.

He was not a strong-minded man; but he had one quality which is almost as valuable a safeguard against temptation as strength of mind—namely, timidity.

His love for his betrothed was chastened by a considerable dash of awe, and he was resolved not to compromise himself in her eyes just for the sake of a little temporary distraction.

At this point of his deliberations he looked

2

at his watch : it was close upon twelve; only
one hour to be got through before tiffin.
Why, an hour was nothing; he could surely
contrive to kill it over Buckle! A little
courage, a little concentration, and he would
certainly attain to an interest in " the laws
which govern human actions."

The ship's bells were just striking; he
counted the strokes: one, two, three, four,
five—and no more! There must be some
mistake; it could not possibly be only half-
past ten. Why, it was hours since breakfast !

" Looking at your watch, eh ? " said his
friend Perkins, as he reached Peter's chair
for about the hundredth time. " Ah ! you're
fast, I see. Haven't altered your watch yet ?
They've put the ship's clock back again this
morning; nearly half an hour it was this
time—it was rather less yesterday and the day
before : we shall go on gaining so much extra
time a day, I suppose, till we get to Gib."

" You don't mean to tell me that! " exclaimed Peter, with a half-suppressed groan.
If the time had seemed tedious and inter-
minable enough before, how much more so

was it now! How infinitely greater would the effort be to fix his thoughts resolutely on Buckle, and ignore the very existence of his distracting neighbors, now that it was to be daily prolonged in this exasperating manner!

"You don't seem to appreciate the arrangement?" remarked the Manager, as he allowed himself to drop cautiously—for he was a bulky man—into a hammock-chair beside Tourmalin.

"Appreciate it!" said Peter, with strong disgust. "Aren't there enough half-hours, and confoundedly long ones, too, in the day as it is, without having extra ones forced on you like this? And giving it to us in the daytime, too! They might at least put the clock back at night, when it wouldn't so much matter. I do think it's very bad management, I must say!"

His companion began a long explanation about the meridian, and sun's time, and ship's time, and Greenwich time, to which Peter gave but a very intermittent attention, so stupefied did he feel at this unwelcome discovery.

"It's a curious thing to think of," the other was saying thoughtfully, "that a man by simply making a voyage like this, should make a clear gain of several hours which he would never have had at all if he had stayed at home!"

"I would much rather be without them," said Peter. "I find it quite difficult enough to spend the time as it is; and how on earth I can spend any more, I don't know!"

"Why spend it, then?" asked his friend quietly.

"What else am I to do with it?"

"What else? See here, my friend; when you have an amount of spare cash that you've no immediate use for, you don't let it lie idle at home, do you? You pay it in to your credit at a bank, and let it remain on deposit till you *do* want it—eh? Well, then, why not treat your spare time as you would your spare cash. Do you see what I mean?"

"Not altogether," confessed Peter, considerably puzzled.

"It's simple enough nowadays. For instance, the establishment I have the honor to be connected with—the Anglo-Australian Joint Stock Time Bank, Limited—confines itself, as you are doubtless aware, almost entirely to that class of business."

"Ah!" said Peter, no more enlightened than before, "does it indeed? Would you mind explaining what particular class of business it carries on? I don't quite understand."

"Bless my soul, sir!" said the Manager, rather irritably, you must be uncommonly ignorant of financial matters not to have heard of this before! However, I will try to make it clear to you. I dare say you have heard that 'Time is money?' Very well, all our operations are conducted on that principle. We are prepared to make advances, on good security of course, of time to almost any amount; and we are simply overwhelmed with applications for loans. Business men, as you may know, are perpetually pressed for time, and will consent to almost anything to obtain it. Our transactions in time, sir, are immense. Why, the amount of Time passing through our books annually during the last ten years, averages—ah! about sixty centuries! That's pretty well, I think, sir?"

He was so perfectly business-like and serious that Peter almost forgot to see anything preposterous in what he said.

"It sounds magnificent," he said politely; "only you see, I don't want to borrow any time myself. I've too much on my hands already."

"Just so," said the Manager; "but if you will kindly hear me out, I am coming to that. Lending time is only one side of our business; we are also ready to accept the charge of any spare time that customers may be willing to deposit with us, and, with our experience and facilities, I need hardly say that we are able to employ it to the best advantage. Now, say, for example, that you wish to open an account with us. Well, we'll take these spare half-hours of yours that are only an encumbrance to you at present, and if you choose to allow them to remain on deposit, they will carry interest at five per cent. per month; that is, five minutes on every hour and three quarters roughly, for each month, until you withdraw them. In that way alone, by merely leaving your time with us for six months you will gain —now, let me see—over three additional hours in compound interest on your original capital of ten hours or so. And no previous notice required before withdrawal! Let me tell you, sir, you will not find many banks do business on such terms as that!"

"No," said Peter, who could not follow all this arithmetic, "so I should imagine. Only, I don't quite see, if you will pardon my saying so, what particular advantage I should gain if I did open an account of this sort."

"You don't? You surprise me, you really do! Here are you, with these additional hours lying idle on your hands; you didn't expect 'em, and don't want 'em. But how do you know that you *mayn't* be glad of 'em at some time or other? Just think how grateful you might be hereafter, if you could get back a single one of these half-hours which you find so tedious now. Half an hour on board a fine ship like this, splendid weather, bracing sea-air, perfect rest, pleasant company, and so on —why, you'd be willing to pay any money for it! Well, bank your extra time ; and you can draw every individual hour in quarters, halves, or wholes, when you please and *as* you please. *That's* the advantage of it, sir !"

"I think I see," said Peter ; "only how am I to make the deposit in the first instance?"

"That's easily arranged. The captain can't

compel you to accept the time now by merely
putting back the hands of the clock, can he?
So all *you* have to do is to abstain from alter-
ing your watch so long as you are on board,
and to fill up a little form; after which I
shall be happy to supply you with a book
of Time Cheques, which you can fill up and
present whenever you wish to spend a given
number of minutes in the pleasantest possible
of ways."

"But where am I to present these cheques?"
inquired Peter.

"Oh!" said the Manager, "there will be
no difficulty whatever about that. Any clock
will cash it for you—provided, of course, that
it hasn't stopped. You merely have to slip
your cheque underneath or behind it, and you
will at once be paid whatever amount of time
the cheque is drawn for. I can show you one
of our forms if you like?"

Here he brought out a bulky leather case,
from which he extracted a printed document,
which he handed to Peter.

Peter, however, being naturally cautious,
felt a hesitation which he scarcely liked to
confess.

"You see," he said, "the fact is, I should
like to know first . . . I've never been engaged
in a—a transaction of this kind before; and,
well—what I mean is, do I incur any risk of
—er—a supernatural character? . . . It isn't
like that business of Faust's, eh, don't you
know?"

The Manager took back the paper with an
abruptness which showed that his temper was
ruffled by this suspicion.

"My good sir!" he said, with a short
offended laugh, "don't, on any account, imagine that *I* care two pins whether you become a depositor or not. I dare say our house
will continue to exist without your account.
As for liability, ours is a limited concern; and,
besides, a deposit would not constitute you
a shareholder. If you meant anything more
—well, I have still to learn that there's anything diabolical about *me*, sir! I simply
thought I was doing you a good turn by making the suggestion; and, besides, as a business
man, I never neglect any opportunity, however small. But it's entirely as you please,
I'm sure."

There was nothing in the least demoniacal,

even in his annoyance, and Peter was moved to contrition and apology.

"I—I really beg your pardon!" he said. "I do hope I haven't offended you; and, if you will allow me, I shall consider it a personal favor to be allowed to open an account with your bank. It would certainly be a great convenience to draw some of this superfluous time at some future day, instead of wasting it now. Where do I sign the form?"

The Manager was appeased; and produced the form once more, indicating the place for the signature, and even providing a stylograph-pen for the purpose. It was still somewhat of a relief to Peter's mind to find that the ink it contained was of the ordinary black hue.

"And now, about cheques," said his friend, after the signature had been obtained. "How many, do you think you would require? I should say that, as the deposit is rather small, you will find fifty more than sufficient? We shall debit you with fifty seconds to cover the cheque-book. And we always recommend 'bearer' cheques as, on the whole, more convenient."

Peter said he would have fifty bearer cheques, and was accordingly given an oblong gray-green book, which, except that it was a trifle smaller, was in nowise different, outwardly, from an ordinary cheque-book. Still, his curiosity was **not** completely satisfied.

"There is just one question more," he said. "When I draw this time, where will it be spent?"

"Why, naturally, on board this ship," explained the Manager. "You see that the time you will get must necessarily be the extra time to which you are entitled by virtue of your passage, and which you *would* have spent as it accrued if you had not chosen to deposit it with us. By the way, when you are filling up cheques, we much prefer not to be called upon to honor drafts for less than fifteen minutes; as much more as you like, but not less. Well, then, we may consider that settled. I am extremely glad to have had the opportunity of obliging you; and I think I can promise that you will have no reason to repent of having made such a use of your time. I'll wish you good-by for the present, sir!"

The Manager resumed his hygienic tramp

round the deck, leaving Peter with the cheque-book in his hand. He was no longer surprised: now that he was more familiar with the idea, it seemed a perfectly natural and matter-of-fact arrangement; he only wondered that he had never thought of so obvious a plan before. And it was an immense relief to know that he had got rid of his extra hours for the present, at all events, and that he could now postpone them to a period at which they would be a boon rather than a burden.

And very soon he put the cheque-book away, and forgot all about it.

THE STORY.

CHAPTER I.

TOURMALIN'S FIRST CHEQUE, AND HOW HE TOOK IT.

Fidelity Rewarded.—Love's Catechism.—Brain-fag.— A Timely Recollection.—The Experiment, and some Startling Results.—Question Time.—" Dear Friends." —A Compromise.

PETER TOURMALIN'S probation was at an end, and, what was more, he had come through the ordeal triumphantly. How he managed this, he scarcely knew; no doubt he was aided by the consciousness that the extra hours which he felt himself most liable to mis-spend had been placed beyond his disposal. At all events, when he met Sophia again, he had been able to convince her that her doubts of his con-

stancy, even under the most trying conditions,
were entirely undeserved. Now he was receiving his recompense : his engagement to
Sophia was no longer conditional, but a recognized and irrevocable fact.   It is superfluous
to say that he was happy.   Sophia had set herself to repair the deficiencies in his education
and culture ; she took him to scientific lectures
and classical concerts, and made him read
standard authors without skipping.   He felt
himself daily acquiring balance and serious-
ness, and an accurate habit of thought, and
all the other qualities which Sophia wished
him to cultivate.

Still, there were moments when he felt the
need of halting and recovering his wind, so
to speak, in the steep and toilsome climb to
her superior mental level—times when he felt
that his overtaxed brain absolutely required
relaxation of some sort.

He felt this particularly one dreary morning, late in November, as he sat in his London
chambers, staring with lack-luster eyes at the
letter he had that day received from his betrothed.   For, although they met nearly every
day, she never allowed one to pass without a

letter—no fond and foolish effusion, be it understood, but a kind of epistolary examination
paper, to test the progress he was making.
This one contained some searching questions
on Buckle's *History of Civilization*, which he
was expected to answer by return of post. He
was not supposed to look at the book, though
he had; and even then he felt himself scarcely
better fitted to floor the tremendous posers de-
vised by Sophia's unwearying care.

The day before, he had had "search-ques-
tions" in English poetry from Chaucer to
Mr. Lewis Morris, which had thinned and
whitened his hair; but this was, if possible,
even worse.

He wished now that he had got up his
Buckle more thoroughly during his voyage on
the *Boomerang*—and, with the name, his arrangement with the manager suddenly rose to
his recollection. What had he done with that
book of Time Cheques? If he could only
get away, if but for a quarter of an hour—
away from those somber rooms, with their
outlook on dingy house-tops and a murky,
rhubarb-colored sky—if he could really exchange all that for the sunniness and warmth

and delicious idleness which had once seemed
so tedious, what a rest it would be! And
would he not return after such an interlude
with all his faculties invigorated, and better
able to cope with the task he now found almost
insuperable?

The first thing was to find the cheque-book,
which did not take him long; though when he
had found it, something made him pause before filling up a cheque. What if he had
been made a fool of—if the Anglo-Australian
Time Cheque Bank never existed, or had suspended payment? But that was easily settled
by presenting a cheque. Why should he not,
just by way of experiment? His balance was
intact as yet; he was never likely to need a
little ready time more than he did just then.
He would draw the minimum amount, fifteen
minutes, and see how the system worked.

So, although he had little real confidence
that anything would happen at all, he drew a
cheque, and slipped it behind the frivolous and
rather incorrect little ormolu clock upon his
chimey-piece.

The result was instantaneous, and altogether
beyond his expectations! The four walls of

his room assumed the transparency of gauze
for a second, before fading entirely away; the
olive fog changed to translucent blue; there
was a briny breath in the air, and he himself
was leaning upon the rail at the forward end
of the hurricane-deck of the *Boomerang*, which
was riding with a slow and stately rise and fall
over the heaving swell.

That was surprising enough; but more surprising still was the discovery that he was apparently engaged in close and confidential conversation with a lovely person in whom he
distinctly recognized Miss Tyrrell.

"Yes, I forgive you, Mr. Tourmalin," she
was saying, with an evident effort to suppress
a certain agitation; but indeed, *indeed*, you
must never speak to me like that again!"

Now, as Peter was certainly not conscious
of ever having spoken to her at all in his life,
this was naturally a startling and even embar-
assing beginning.

But he had presence of mind enough to
take in the position of affairs, and adapt himself to them. This was one of the quarters of
an hour he *would* have had, and it was clear
that in some portion or other of his spare

3

time he would have made Miss Tyrrell's acquaintance in some way. Of course he ought to have been paid that particular time first; but he could easily see from her manner, and the almost tender friendliness which shone in her moistened eyes, that at this period they had advanced considerably beyond mere acquaintanceship. There had been some little mistake probably; the cheques had been wrongly numbered perhaps, or else they were honored without regard to chronological sequence, which was most confusing.

Still, he had nothing to do but conceal his ignorance as well as he could, and pick up the loose threads as he went along. He was able, at all events, to assure her that he would not, if he could help it, incur her displeasure by speaking to her " like that " in future.

"Thanks," she said. " I know it was only a temporary forgetfulness; and—and if what you suspect should prove to be really true— why, then, Mr. Tourmalin, then, of course, you may come and tell me so."

"I will," he said. "I shall make a point of it. Only," he thought to himself, "she will have to tell me first *what* I'm to tell her."

" And in the mean time," she said, " let us go on as before, as if you had never brought yourself to confide your sad story to me."

So he had told a sad story, had he? he thought, much bewildered; for, as he had no story belonging to him of that character, he was afraid he must have invented one, while, of course, he could not ask for information.

" Yes," he said, with great presence of mind, " forget my unhappy story—let it never be mentioned between us again. We will go on as before—*exactly* as before."

" It is our only course," she agreed. " And now," she added, with a cheerfulness that struck him as a little forced, " suppose we talk of something else."

Peter considered this a good suggestion, provided it was a subject he knew a little more about; which, unhappily, it was not.

" You never answered my question," she reminded him.

He would have liked, as Ministers say in the House, " previous notice of that question;" but he could hardly say so in so many words.

" No," he said. " Forgive me if I say that it is a—a painful subject to me."

"I understand that," she said gently (it was more than *he* did); "but tell me only this: was it *that* that made you behave as you did? You are sure you had no *other* reason?"

["If I said I had," thought Peter, "she will ask me what it was."] "I will be as frank as possible, Miss Tyrrell," he replied. "I had *no* other reason. What other reason *could* I have had?"

"I half fancied—but I ought to have seen from the first that, whatever it was, it was not that. And now you have made everything quite clear."

"I am glad you find it so," said Peter, with a touch of envy.

"But I might have gone on misunderstanding and misjudging, putting you down as proud and cold and unsociable, or prejudiced, but for the accident which brought us together, in spite of your determination that we should remain total strangers."

It was an *accident* which had made them acquainted, then. He would draw the cheque which contained that episode of his extra time sooner or later; but it was distinctly inconvenient not to have at least *some* idea of what had happened.

"A fortunate accident for me, at all events," he said with a judicious recourse to compliment.

"It might have been a very unfortunate one for poor papa," she said, "but for you. I do believe he would have been quite inconsolable."

Peter felt an agreeable shock. Had he really been fortunate enough to distinguish himself by rescuing the Judge's fair daughter from some deadly peril? It looked very like it. He had often suspected himself of a latent heroism which had never had an opportunity of being displayed. This opportunity must have occurred, and he have proved equal to the occasion, in one of those extra hours!

"I can quite imagine that he would be inconsolable indeed!" he said gallantly. "Fortunately, I was privileged to prevent such a calamity."

"Tell me again exactly *how* you did it," she said. "I never quite understood."

Peter again took refuge in a discreet vagueness.

"Oh," he replied, modestly, "there is not much to tell. I saw the—er—danger, and knew there wasn't a moment to lose; and then I sprang forward, and—well, you know the rest as well as I do!"

"You only just caught him as he was going up the rigging, didn't you?" she asked.

So it was the Judge he had saved—not his daughter! Peter felt a natural disappointment. But he saw the state of the case now: a powerful judicial intellect over-strained, melancholia, suicidal impulses—it was all very sad; but happily he had succeeded in saving this man to his country.

"I—ventured to detain him," he said, considerately, "seeing that he was—er—rather excited."

"But weren't you afraid he would bite you?"

"No," said Peter, pained at this revelation of the Judge's condition, "that possibility did *not* occur to me. In fact I am sure that—er—though the strongest intellects are occasionally subject to attacks of this sort, he would never so far forgot himself as to—er—bite a complete stranger."

"Ah!" she said, "you don't know what a

savage old creature he can be sometimes. He never ought to be let loose; I'm sure he's dangerous!"

"Oh! but think, Miss Tyrrell," remonstrated Peter, unmistakably shocked at this unfilial attitude toward a distinguished parent; "if he was—er—dangerous, he would not be upon the Bench now, surely!"

She glanced over her shoulder with evident apprehension.

"How you frightened me!" she said. "I thought he was really there! But I hope they'll shut him up in future, so that he won't be able to do any more mischief. You didn't tell me how you got hold of him. Was it by his chain or his tail?"

Peter did not know; and, besides, it was as difficult for him to picture himself in the act of seizing a hypochondriacal judge by his watch-chain or coat-tail, as it was for him to comprehend the utter want of feeling that could prompt such a question from the sufferer's own daughter.

"I hope," he said, with a gravity which he intended as a rebuke—"I hope I treated him with all the respect and consideration possible

under the—er—circumstances. . . . I am sorry
that that remark appears to amuse you ! "

For Miss Tyrrell was actually laughing, with
a merriment in which there was nothing
forced.

" How can I help it? " she said, as soon
as she could speak. " It is too funny to hear
you talking of being regretful and considerate
to a horrid monkey ! "

" A *monkey !* " he repeated involuntarily.

So it was a monkey that was under restraint
and not a Judge of her Majesty's Supreme
Court of Judicature ; a discovery which left
him as much in the dark as to what particular
service he had rendered as ever, and made
him tremble to think what he might have
said. But apparently, by singular good fortune, he had not committed himself beyond
recovery ; for Miss Tyrrell only said :

" I thought you were speaking of the monkey, the little wretch that came up behind papa
and snatched away all his notes—the notes
he had made for the great case he tried last
term, and has to deliver judgment upon when
the Courts sit again. Surely he told you how
important they were, and how awkward it

would have been if the monkey had escaped
with them, and torn them into pieces or dropped
them into the sea ?—as he probably would have
done but for you ! "

" Oh, ah, yes ! " said Peter, feeling slightly
crest-fallen, for he had hoped he had per-
formed a more dashing deed than catching a
loose monkey. " I believe your father—Sir
John ? " he hazarded . . . " Sir William, of
course, thank you . . . did mention the fact.
But it really was such a trifling thing to do."

" Papa didn't think so," she said. " He de-
clares he can never be grateful enough to you.
And, whatever it was," she added softly, and
even shyly, " I, at least, can never think lightly
of a service which has—has made us what we
are to one another."

What they were to one another ! And
what was *that ?* A dreadful uncertainty
seized upon Peter. Was it possible that, in
some way he did not understand, he was engaged to this very charming girl, who was
almost a stranger to him? The mere idea
froze his blood ; for if that was so, how did
it affect his position toward Sophia? At all
hazards, he must know the worst at once !

"Tell me," he said with trembling accents,—
"I know you have told me already, but tell me
once more—precisely what we are to one an.
other at present. It would be so much more
satisfactory to my mind," he added, in a de-
precatory tone, "to have that clearly understood."

"I thought I had made it quite clear already," she said, with the least suspicion of
coldness, "that we can be nothing more to one
another than friends."

The relief was almost too much for him.
What a dear, good, sensible girl she was!
How perfectly she appreciated the facts!

"*Friends!*" he cried. "Is that *all?* Do
you really mean we are nothing more than
friends?"

He caught her hand, in the fervor of his
gratitude, and she allowed it to remain in his
grasp; which in the altered state of things,
he found rather pleasant than otherwise.

"Ah!" she murmured, "don't ask me for
more than I have said—more than I can ever
say, perhaps! Let us be content with remaining friends—dear friends, if you like—but no
more!"

"I will," said Peter promptly, "I will be content. Dear friends, by all means; but no more!"

"No," she assented; "unless a time should come when—"

"Yes," said Peter, encouragingly, as she hesitated. "You were about to say, a time when—?"

Her lips moved, a faint flush stole into her cheeks; she was about to complete her sentence, when her hand seemed to melt away in his own, and he stood, grasping the empty air, by his own mantelpiece. The upper deck, the heaving bows, the blue seaboard, Miss Tyrrell herself, all had vanished; and in their stead were the familiar surroundings of his chamber, the grimy London housefronts, and Sophia's list of questions lying still unanswered upon his writing-table! His fifteen minutes had come to an end; the cheque was nowhere to be seen. The minute-hand of his clock had not moved since he last saw it; but this last circumstance, as he saw on reflection, was only natural, for otherwise the Time Deposit would have conferred no real advantage, as he would never have regained the hours he had temporarily foregone.

For some time Peter sat perfectly still, with his head between his hands, occupied in a mental review of this his initial experience of the cheque-book system. It was as different as possible from the spell of perfect rest he had anticipated; but had it been unpleasant on that account? In spite of an element of mystification at starting, which was inevitable, he was obliged to admit to himself that he had enjoyed this little adventure more than perhaps he should have done. With all his attachment to Sophia, he could hardly be insensible to the privilege of suddenly finding himself the friend—and more than that, the dear friend—of so delightful a girl as this Miss Tyrrell.

There was a strange charm, a peculiar and quite platonic tenderness about an intimacy of this peculiar and unprecedented nature, which increased at every fresh recollection of it. It increased so rapidly indeed, that almost unconsciously he drew the cheque-book toward him, and began to fill up another cheque with a view to an immediate return to the *Boomerang.*

But when he had torn the cheque out, he

hesitated. It was all quite harmless: the most
severe moralist could not convict him of even
the most shadowy infidelity toward his *fiancée*,
if he chose to go back and follow up a purely
retrospective episode like this—an episode
which interested and fascinated him so strongly
—only, what would Sophia say to it? In-
stinctively he felt that the situation, innocent
as it was, would fail to commend itself to her.
He had no intention of informing her, it was
true; but he knew that he was a poor dis-
sembler—he might easily betray himself in
some unguarded moment, and then— No!
it was vexing, no doubt; but upon the whole,
it was wiser and better to renounce those additional hours on board the *Boomerang* altogether—to allow this past, that never had, but
only might have been, to remain unsummoned
and unknown forever. Otherwise, who could
tell that, by gradual assaults, even such an affection as he had for Sophia might not be
eventually undermined.

But this fear, as he saw the next moment,
was almost too extravagant to be seriously
taken into account. He felt nothing, and
never could feel anything, but warm and sin-

cere friendship for Miss Tyrrell; and it was
satisfactory to know that she was in no danger
of mistaking his sentiments. Still, of course
there was always a certain risk, particularly
when he was necessarily in ignorance of all
that had preceded and followed the only col-
loquy they had had as yet. At last he decided
upon a compromise: he would not cash that
second cheque for the present, at all events;
he would reserve it for an emergency, and
only use it if he was absolutely driven to do so
as a mental tonic. Perhaps Sophia would not
compel him to such a necessity again; he
hoped—at least he *thought* she would not.

So he put the unpresented cheque in an in-
ner pocket, and set to work with desperate
energy at his examination-paper; although
his recent change must have proved less stimulating to his jaded faculties than he had hoped,
since Sophia, after reading his answers, made
the cutting remark that she scarcely knew
which he had more completely failed to
apprehend—the purport of his author, or
that of the very simple questions she had
set him.

Peter could not help thinking, rather ruefully, that Miss Tyrrell would never have been capable of such severity as that; but, then, Miss Tyrrell was not his *fiancée*, only a very dear friend, whom he would, most probably, never meet again.

CHAPTER II.

THE SECOND CHEQUE.

*Furnishing.—A Cosy Corner.—" Sitting Out."—Fresh
Discoveries.— Twice a Hero.— Bewilderment and
Bathos.*

THE knowledge that one has a remedy within reach is often as effectual as the remedy itself, if not more so; which may account for
the fact that, although a considerable number
of weeks had elapsed since Peter Tourmalin
had drawn his second cheque on the Anglo-
Australian Joint Stock Time Bank, that cheque
still remained unpresented.

The day fixed for his wedding with Sophia
was drawing near; the flat in the Marylebone
Road, which was to be the scene of their joint
felicity, had to be furnished, and this occupied
most of his time. Sophia took the entire business upon herself, for she had scientific theo-

ries on the subject of decoration and color har-
monies which Peter could only accept with
admiring awe; but, nevertheless, she required
him to be constantly at hand, so that she could
consult him after her own mind had been ir-
revocably made up.

One February afternoon he was wandering
rather disconsolately about the labyrinthine
passages of one of the monster upholstery es-
tablishments in the Tottenham Court Road, his
chief object being to evade the courtesies of
the numerous assistants as they anxiously inquired what they might have the pleasure of
showing him. He and Sophia had been there
since midday; and she had sat in judgment
upon carpets which were brought out, plunging like unbroken colts, by panting foremen,
and unrolled before her in a blinding riot of
color. Peter had only to express the mildest
commendation of any carpet to seal that carpet's doom instantly; so that he soon abstained
from personal interference.

Now Sophia was in the ironmongery department, choosing kitchen utensils, and his
opinion being naturally of no value on such
matters, he was free to roam wherever he

4

pleased within the limits of the building. He felt tired and rather faint, for he had had no lunch; and presently he came to a series of show-rooms fitted up as rooms in various styles: there was one inviting-looking interior, with an elaborate chimneypiece which had cosy cushioned nooks on either side of the fireplace, and into one of these corners he sank with heartfelt gratitude; for it was a comfortable seat, and he had not sat down for hours. But as his weariness wore away, he felt the want of something to occupy his mind, and searched in his pockets to see if he had any letters there—even notes of congratulation upon his approaching marriage would be better than nothing in his present reduced condition. But he had left all his correspondence at his chambers. The only document he came upon was the identical time cheque he had drawn long ago: it was creased and rumpled; but none the less negotiable, if he could find a clock. And on the built-up chimneypiece there was a clock, a small *faience* affair surmounted by a Japanese monster in peacock-blue. Moreover, by some chance, this clock was actually going—he could hear it ticking as he sat there. Should he present his cheque or not; he was feeling a little aggrieved at Sophia's treatment of him, she had snubbed him so unmercifully over the carpets; it was pleasant to think that, if he chose, he could transport himself that very instant to the society of a sweet and appreciative companion from whom snubbing was the last thing to be apprehended.

Yes; Sophia's treatment quite justified him in making an exception to the rule he had laid down for himself — he *would* present that cheque. And he rose softly from his seat and pushed the cheque under the little time-piece. . . .

As before, his draft was honored immediately; he found himself on a steamer-chair in a sheltered passage between two of the deck-cabins. It was night, and he could not clearly distinguish any objects around him for some little time, owing to the darkness; but from a glimmer of white drapery that was faintly visible close by, he easily inferred that there was another chair adjoining his, which could only be occupied by Miss Tyrrell. He could just hear the ship's band playing a waltz at the further end of the ship; it was one of the evenings when there had been dancing, and he and Miss Tyrrell were sitting out together.

All this he realized instantly, and not without a thrill of interest and expectation, which, however, the first words she uttered were sufficient to reduce to the most prosaic perplexity.

"What have I said?" she was moaning, in a voice hardly recognizable from emotion and the fleecy wrap in which her face was muffled —"oh! what *have* I said?"

Peter was naturally powerless to afford her any information on this point, even if she really required it; he made a rapid mental note to the effect that their intimacy had evidently made great progress since their last interview.

"I'm afraid," he said, deciding that candor was his only course, "I can't exactly tell you what you did say; for, as a matter of fact, I didn't quite catch it."

"Ah! you say that to spare me," she murmured; "you *must* have heard; but, promise me you will forget it?"

"Willingly," said Peter, with the greatest readiness to oblige; "I will consider it forgotten."

"If I could but hope that!" she said. "And, yet," she added recklessly, "why should I care what I say?"

"To be sure," agreed Tourmalin at random, "why *should* you, you know?"

"You must have seen from the first that I was very far from being happy?"

"I must confess," said Peter, with the air of a man whom nothing escaped, "that I *did* observe that."

"And you were right! Was it unnatural that I should be nothing but grateful to the chance which first brought us together?"

"Not at all," said Peter, delighted to feel himself on solid ground again; "indeed, if I may speak for myself, I have even greater reason to feel grateful to that monkey."

"To *what* monkey?" she exclaimed.

"Why, naturally, my dear Miss Tyrrell, to the animal which was the unconscious instrument in making us acquainted. You surely can not have forgotten already that it *was* a monkey?"

She half rose with an impetuous movement, the mantilla fell from her face, and even in the faint starlight, he could perceive that, beautiful as that face undoubtedly was, it was as certainly not the face of Miss Tyrrell!

" *You* seem to have forgotten a great deal," she retorted, with a suppressed sob in her voice, " or you would at least remember that my name is Davenport. Why you should choose to call me Miss Tyrrell, whom I don't even know by sight, I can't conceive ! "

Here was a discovery, and a startling one! It appeared that he had not merely one, but two dear friends on board this P. and O. steamer ; and the second seemed, if possible, even dearer than the first! He must have made the very most of those extra hours !

There was one comfort, however, Miss Davenport did not, contrary to his impression, know Miss Tyrrell ; so that they need not necessarily clash—still, it was undeniably awkward. He had to get out of his mistake as well as he could, which was but lamely.

" Why, of *course*," he protested, " I know *you* are Miss Davenport. Most stupid of me to address you as Miss Tyrrell ! The—the only explanation I can offer is, that before I had the pleasure of speaking to you, I was under the impression that your proper name was *Tyrrell*, and so it slipped out again just then from habit."

This—though the literal, if not the moral, truth—did not seem to satisfy her entirely.

"That may be so," she said, curtly; "still it does not explain why you should address me as *Miss* Anybody, after asking and receiving permission, only last night, to call me by my Christian name!"

Obviously their relations were even closer than he had imagined. He had no idea they had got as far as Christian names already, any more than he had of what hers might happen to be.

There was a painful want of method in the manner this Time Bank conducted its business, as he could not help remarking to himself; however, Peter, perhaps, from the very timidity in his character, developed unexpected adroitness in a situation of some difficulty.

"So you did!" he said. "You allowed me to call you by your—er—Christian name; but I value such a privilege too highly to use it—er—indiscriminately."

"You are very strange to-night!" she said, with a plaintive and almost childish quiver of the lip. "First you call me 'Miss Tyrrell' and then 'Miss Davenport,' and then you will have it that we were introduced by a monkey! As if I should ever allow a monkey to introduce *anybody* to me! Is saving a girl's life such an ordinary event with you, that you forget all about such a trifle?"

This last sentence compensated Peter for all that had gone before. Here was a person whose life he really *had* saved; and his heart warmed to her from that moment. Rescuing a girl from imminent bodily peril was a more heroic achievement than capturing the most mischievous of monkeys; and, besides, he felt it was far more in his style. So it was in his best manner he replied to her question:

"It would be strange, indeed," he said reproachfully, "If I could ever forget that I was the humble means of preserving you from—from a watery grave"—(he risked the epithet, concluding that on a voyage it could hardly be any other description of grave; and she did not challenge it, so he continued)—"a watery grave; but I *had* hoped you would appreciate the motive which restrained me from—er—seeming to dwell upon such a circumstance."

This appeal, unprincipled as it was, subdued her instantly.

"Oh, forgive me!" she said, putting out her hand with the prettiest penitence. "I might have known you better than that. I didn't mean it. Please say you forgive me, and—and call me Maud again!"

Relief at being supplied with a missing clew made Peter reckless; indeed, it is to be feared that demoralization had already set in; he took the hand she gave him, and it did not occur to him to let it go immediately.

"Maud, then," he said obediently; "I forgive you, Maud."

It was a prettier name to pronounce than Sophia.

"How curious it is," she was saying, dreamily, as she nestled comfortably in her chair beside him, "that, up to the very moment when you rushed forward that day, I scarcely gave your existence a thought! And now—how little we ever know what is going to happen to us, do we?"

["Or what *has* happened, for that matter!" he thought.] This time he would not commit himself to details until he could learn more about the precise nature of his dauntless act, which he at once proceeded to do.

"I should very much like to know," he suggested, "what your sensations were at that critical moment."

"My sensations? I hardly know," she said, "I remember leaning over the—bulwarks, is it?" (Peter said it *was* bulwarks)—"the bulwarks, watching a sailor in a little balcony below, who was doing something with a long line—"

"Heaving the lead," said Peter; "so he was—go on!"

He was intensely excited; it was all plain enough: she had lost her balance and fallen overboard; he had plunged in, and gallantly kept her above water till help arrived. He had always known he was capable of this sort of thing; now he had proved it.

"—When all at once," she continued, "I felt myself roughly dragged back by somebody —that was you! I was rather angry for the moment, for it *did* seem quite a liberty for a total stranger to take,—when, that very instant, I saw the line with a great heavy lump of lead at the end of it whirled round exactly where my head had been, and then I knew that I owed my life to your presence of mind!"

Peter was more than disappointed—he was positively disgusted at this exceedingly tame conclusion; it *did* seem hard that, even under conditions when any act of daring might have been possible to him, he could do nothing more brilliant than this. It was really worse than the monkey business!

"I'm afraid you make too much of the very little I did," he said.

"Do I? Perhaps that is because if you had not done it, we should never come to know one another as we do!" (So far, it was a very one-sided sort of knowledge, Peter thought.) "And yet," she added, with a long-drawn sigh, "I sometimes think that we should both be happier if we never *had* known one another; if you had stood aside, and the lead had struck me and I had died!"

"No, no!" said Peter, unfeignedly alarmed at this morbid reflection, "you mustn't take such a gloomy view of it as all that, you know!"

"Why not?" she said, in a somber tone.

"It *is* gloomy—*how* gloomy I know better than you!" ("She might well do that," thought Tourmalin.) "Why did I not see that I was slowly, imperceptibly drifting—drifting?"

"Well," said Peter, with a levity he was far from feeling, "if the drifting was imperceptible, you naturally *wouldn't* see it, you know!"

"You might have spared a joke at such a time as this!" she cried, indignantly.

"I—I wasn't aware there was a close time for jokes," he said, humbly; "not that it was much of a joke!"

"Indeed it was not," she replied. "But oh, Peter, *now* we have both drifted!" "Have we?" he exclaimed, blankly. "I—I mean—*haven't* we!"

"I was so blind—so willfully, foolishly blind! I told myself we were friends!"

"Surely we are?" he said retaking possession of her hand; he had entirely forgotten Sophia in the ironmongery department, at Tottenham Court Road. "I—I understood we were on that footing?"

"No," she said, "let us have no subterfuges any more—we must look facts in the face.

After what we have both said to-night, we can no longer deceive ourselves by words. . . . Peter," she broke off suddenly, "I am going to ask you a question, and on your answer my fate—and yours too, perhaps—will depend! Tell me truthfully . . ." Her voice failed her for the moment, as she bent over toward him, and clutched his arm tightly in her excitement; her eyes shone with a wild, intense eagerness for his reply. . . . "Would you—" she repeated . . .

"Would you have the bottle-jack all brass, or japanned? The brass ones are a shilling more."

Peter gave a violent start, for the voice in which this most incongruous and irrelevant question was put was that of Sophia!

Miss Davenport with her hysterical appeal, the steamer-chairs, and the starlight, all had fled, and he stood, supporting himself limply by the arm of the chimney-nook in the upholsterer's showroom, staring at Sophia, who stood there, sedate and practical, inviting his attention to a couple of bottle-jacks which an assistant was displaying with an obsequious smile: the transition was rather an abrupt one.

"Oh, I think the brass one is very nice," he stammered, feebly enough.

"Then that settles it," remarked Sophia; "we'll take the *japanned* one, please," she said to the assistant.

"Aren't you feeling well, Peter dear?" she asked presently, in an undertone. "You look so odd!"

"Quite well," he said; "I—ah!—was thinking of something else for the moment, and you startled me, that's all."

"You had such a far-away expression in your eyes," said Sophia, "and you did jump so when I spoke to you; you should really try to conquer that tendency to let yourself wander, Peter."

"I will, my love," he said; and he meant it, for he had let himself wander farther than he quite intended.

CHAPTER III.

Good Resolutions.—Casuistry.— A Farewell Visit.— Small Profit and a Quick Return.

As the reader may imagine, this second experience had an effect upon Peter that was rather deterrent than encouraging.

It was a painful piece of self-revelation to find that, had he chosen to avail himself of the extra hours on board the *Boomerang* as they occurred, he would have so employed them as to place himself in relations of considerable ambiguity toward two distinct young ladies. How far he was committed to either, or both, he could not tell; but he had an uneasy suspicion that neither of them would have been quite so emotional had he conducted himself with the same prudence that had marked his behavior throughout the time which he *was* able to account for.

And yet his conscience acquitted him of any actual default; if he had ever really had any passages at all approaching the sentimental with either Miss Tyrrell or Miss Davenport, his mind could hardly be so utterly blank on the subject as it certainly was. No; at the worst, his failings were only potential peccadilloes, the kind of weaknesses he might have given way to if he had not wisely postponed the hours in which the occasions were afforded.

He had had a warning, a practical moral lesson which had merely arrived, as such things often do, rather after date.

But, so far as it was possible to profit by it, he would: at least, he would abstain from making any further inroads upon the balance of extra time which still remained to his credit at the bank; he would draw no further cheques; he would return to that P. and O. steamer no more. For an engaged man whose wedding-day was approaching by leaps and bounds, it was, however innocent, too disturbing and exciting a form of distraction to be quite safely indulged in.

The resolution cost him something, nevertheless. Peter was not a man who had hitherto been spoiled by feminine adoration. Sophia was fond of him, but she never affected to place him upon any sort of pinnacle; on the contrary, she looked down upon him protectingly and indulgently from a moral and intellectual pedestal of her own. He had not objected to this, in fact he rather liked it, but it was less gratifying and stimulating to his self-esteem than the romantic and idealizing sentiments which he had seemingly inspired in two exceedingly bewitching young persons with whom he felt so much in sympathy. It was an agreeable return from the bread-and-butter of engaged life to the *petits fours* of semi-flirtation. After all, Peter was but human, and a man is seldom esteemed for being otherwise. He could not help a natural regret at having to abandon experiences which, judging from the fragmentary samples he had obtained, promised so much and such varied interest. That the interest was not consecutive, only made it the more amusing—it was a living puzzle-picture, the pieces of which he could fit together as he received them. It was tantaliz-

5

ing to look at his cheque-book and feel that
upon its leaves the rest of the story was written, but that he must never seek to decipher
it: it became so tantalizing, that he locked
the cheque-book up at last.

But already some of the edge had worn off
his resolution, and he had begun to see only
the more seductive side of interviews which
at the time, had not been free from difficulty
and embarrassment. Having put himself beyond the reach of temptation, he naturally
began to cast about for some excuse for again
exposing himself to it.

It was the eve of his wedding-day; he was
in his chambers for the last time and alone,
for he would not see Sophia again until he met
her in bridal array at the church door, and he
had no bachelor friends whom he cared to in-
vite to help him to keep up his spirits.

Peter was horribly restless and nervous; he
needed a sedative of some kind, and even trying on his wedding garments failed to soothe
him, as he felt almost certain there was a
wrinkle between the shoulders, and it was too
late to have it altered.

The idea of one more visit to the *Boomer-*

any—one more interview, the last, with one or other of his amiable and fascinating friends —it did not matter very much which—presented itself in a more and more attractive light. If it did nothing else, it would provide him with something to think about for the rest of the evening.

Was it courteous, was it even right, to drop his friends without the slightest apology or explanation? Ought he not, as a gentleman and a man of honor, to go back and bid them " Good-by ? " Peter, after carefully considering the point, discovered that it was clearly his duty to perform this trifling act of civility.

As soon as he had settled that, he got out his cheque-book from the dispatch-box, in which he had placed it for his own security, and, sitting down just as he was, drew another fifteen minutes, and cashed them, like the first, at the ormolu clock. . . .

This time he found himself sitting on a cushioned bench in the music-room of the *Boomerang.* It was shortly after sunset, as he could tell from the bar of dusky crimson against the violet sea, which, framed in the ports opposite, rose and sank with each roll of

the ship. There was a swell on, and she
rolled more than he could have wished.

As he expected, he was not alone; but, as
he had *not* expected, his companion was neither
Miss Tyrrell nor Miss Davenport, but a grim
and portly matron, who was eyeing him with
a look of strong disfavor, which made Peter
wish he had not come. "What," he wondered, "was he in for now?" His uneasiness
was increased as he glanced down upon his
trousers, which, being new and of a delicate
lavender tint, reminded him that in his impatience he had come away in his wedding garments. He feared that he must present rather
an odd appearance on board ship in this festal
attire; but there he would have to stay for
the next quarter of an hour, and he must make
the best of it.

"I repeat, Mr. Tourmalin," said the matron,
"you are doubtless not unprepared for the
fact that I have requested a few minutes'
private conversation with you?"

"Pardon me," said Peter, quaking already
at this alarming opening, "but I am—very
much unprepared." "Surely," he thought,
"this could not be *another* dear friend? No,

that was too absurd—he must have drawn the line *somewhere!*"

"Then permit me to enlighten you," she said raspingly. "I sent for you at a time when we are least likely to be interrupted, to demand an explanation from you upon a very delicate and painful matter which has recently come to my knowledge."

"*Oh!*" said Peter—and nothing more. He guessed her purpose at once; she was going to ask him his intentions with regard to her daughter! He could have wished for some indication as to whether she was Lady Tyrrell or Mrs. Davenport; but, as he had none at present, "Oh" seemed the safest remark to make.

"Life on board a large passenger-ship, Mr. Tourmalin," she went on to observe, "though relaxed in some respects, is still not without decencies which a gentleman is bound to respect."

"Quite so," said Peter, unable to discover the bearings which lay in the application of this particular observation.

"You *say* 'Quite so'; but what has your *behavior* been, sir?"

"That," said Peter, "is exactly what I should like to know myself!"

"A true gentleman would have considered the responsibility he incurred by giving currency to idle and malicious gossip!"

His apprehensions were correct then: it *was* one of the young ladies' mothers—but *which ?*

"I can only assure you, madam," he began, " that if unhappily I have—er—been the means of furnishing gossip, it has been entirely unintentional."

She seemed so much mollified by this, that he proceeded with more confidence :

"As to anything I may have said to your daughter —" when she almost bounded from her seat with fury.

"My *daughter*, sir! Do you mean to sit there and tell me that you had the audacity to so much as hint of such a thing to my daughter, of all people ? "

" So—so much depends on who your daughter is ! " said Peter, completely losing his head.

"You dared to strike this cruel and unmanly blow at the self-respect of a sensitive girl—to poison her defenseless ears with your false, dastardly insinuations—and you can actually admit it?"

"I don't know whether I can admit it or not yet," he replied. "And—and you do put things so very strongly! It is like this: if you are referring to any conversation I may have had with Miss Tyrrell—"

"*Miss Tyrrell?* You have told her *too!*" exclaimed this terrible old matron, thereby demonstrating that, at least, she was not Lady Tyrrell.

"I—I *should* have said Miss Davenport," said Peter, correcting himself precipitately.

"Miss Davenport as well? Upon my word! And pray, sir, may I ask how many other ladies on board this ship are in possession of your amiable confidences?"

He raised his hands in utter despair.

"I can't say," he groaned. "I don't really know what I may have said, or whom I may have said it to! I—I seem to have done so much in my spare time, but I never meant anything!"

"It may be so," she said; "indeed, you hardly seem to me accountable for your actions, or you would not appear in such a ridiculous costume as that, with a sprig of orange-blossom in your button-hole and a high hat, too!"

"I quite feel," said Peter, blushing, "that such a costume must strike you as inappropriate; but—but I happened to be trying them on, and—rather than keep you waiting—"

"Well, well, sir, never mind your costume—the question is, if you are genuinely anxious to repair the wrong you have done, what course do you propose to take?"

"I will be perfectly frank with you, madam," said Peter: "I am not in a position to repair any wrong I have done—if I *have* done any wrong (which I don't admit)—by taking any course whatever!"

"You are *not!*" she cried. "And you tell me so to my face?"

After all, reflected Peter, why should he be afraid of this old lady? In a few more minutes he would be many hundreds of miles away, and he would take very good care not to come back again. He felt master of the situation, and determined to brazen it out.

"I do, madam!" he said, crossing his legs in an easy fashion. "Look at it from a reasonable point of view. There is safety in numbers; and if I have been so unfortunate as to give several young ladies here an entirely erroneous impression, I must leave it to you to undeceive them as considerately but distinctly as you can. For me to make any selection would only create ill-feeling among the rest; and their own good sense will show them that I am forbidden by the laws of my country, which I am the last person to set at defiance—that I am forbidden (even if I were free in other respects, which I am not) to marry them all!"

"The only possible explanation of your conduct is, that you are not in your right mind!" she said. "Who in the world spoke or dreamed of your marrying any one of them? Certainly not *I!*"

"Oh!" said Peter, hopelessly fogged once more. "I thought I might unintentionally have given them grounds for some such expectation. I'm very glad I was mistaken. You see, you must really make allowances for my utter ignorance."

"If this idiotic behavior is not a mere feint, sir, I can make allowances for much; but, surely, you are at least sufficiently in your proper senses to see how abominably you have behaved?"

" Have I?" said Peter, submissively. " I don't wish to contradict you, if you say so, I'm sure. And, as I have some reason to believe that my stay on board this ship will not last very much longer, I should like before I go to express my very sincere regret."

" There is an easy way of proving your sincerity, sir, if you choose to avail yourself of it," she said. " I find it very difficult to believe, from the evident feebleness of your intellect, that you can be the person chiefly responsible for this scandal. Am I correct in my supposition?"

" You are, madam," said Peter. " I should never have got myself into such a tangle as this, if I had not been talked over by Mr. Perkins. I don't know if I can succeed in making myself clear, for the whole business is rather complicated ; but I can try to explain it, if you will only have a little patience."

" You have said quite enough," she said.

"I know all I wish to know now. So it was Mr. Perkins who has been using you as his instrument, was it?"

" Certainly," said Peter ; " but for him, nothing of this would have happened."

" You will have no objection to repeating that statement, should I call upon you to do so?"

" No," said Peter, who observed with pleasure that her wrath against himself was almost entirely moderated ; " but you will have to call *soon*, or I shall have gone. I—I don't know if I shall have another opportunity of meeting Mr. Perkins ; but if I did, I should certainly tell him that I do *not* consider he has treated me quite fairly. He has put me in what I may call a false position, in *several* false positions ; and if I had had the knowledge I have now, I should have had nothing to do with him from the first. He entirely misled me over this business ! "

" Very well, sir," she said ; " you have shown a more gentlemanly spirit, on the whole, than I expected. I am glad to find that your evil has been wrought more by want of thought than heart. It will be for you to complete

your reparation when the proper time arrives.
In the mean time, let this be a warning to you,
sir, never to—" . . .

But here Peter made the sudden discovery
that he was no longer in the music-room of
the *Boomerang*, but at home in his old easy-
chair by his bachelor fireside.

"Phew!" he muttered to himself, "that
was a bad quarter of an hour while it lasted!
What an old she-dragon it was! But she's
right—it *is* a warning to me. I mustn't—I
really must *not* draw any more of these confounded time cheques. I've made that ship
too hot to hold me already! I'd better remain
forever in contented ignorance of how I spent
that extra time, than to go on getting into one
mess after another like this! It was a wonder
I got out of this one as well as I did; but evidently that old woman knew what Perkins is,
and saw *I* wasn't to blame. Now she'll explain the whole affair to all those girls (whoever they may be), and pitch into Perkins—
and serve him right! *I'm* out of it, at any
rate; and now, thank goodness, after to-morrow
I shall have nothing to do but live contentedly
and happily with dearest Sophia! I'd better

burn this beastly cheque-book—I shall never want it again!"

It would have been well for Peter if he had burned that cheque-book; but when it came to the point, he could not bring himself to destroy it. After all, it was an interesting *souvenir* of some very curious, if not unique, experiences; and, as such, he decided to preserve it.

CHAPTER IV.

THE FOURTH CHEQUE.

A Blue Moon.—Felicity in a Flat.—Practical Astronomy.—Temptation and a Relapse.—The Difficulties of being Completely Candid.—A Slight Misunderstanding.—The Avenging Orange.

PETER TOURMALIN enjoyed his honeymoon extremely, in a calm, sober, and rational manner. Sophia discouraged rapture; but, on the other hand, no one was better fitted to inspire and sustain an intelligent interest in the wonders of Geology; and, catching her scientific enthusiasm, Peter spent many happy hours with her along the cliffs, searching for fossil remains. In fact, the only cloud that threatened to mar their felicity at all was an unfortunate tendency on his part to confuse a trilobite with a graptolite, a blunder for which Sophia had no tolerance. He was hazy about his

periods, too, until she sent up to town for
Lyell's great work on the subject as a birth-
day surprise for him, and he read it aloud to
her on the sands. Altogether, it was a peaceful, happy time.

And never once in the whole course of his
honeymoon did he seriously entertain the possibility of making any further use of his book
of blank Time Cheques. If he had contemplated it, no harm would have been done, however, as the book was lying among his neglected
papers at his former chambers.

He felt no poignant regret when the month
came to an end, and they returned to town to
take possession of their Marylebone flat: for
what was it but shifting the scene of their
happiness? And after this had taken place,
Peter was still too much occupied to have leis-
ure for idle and mischievous thoughts. Marrying Sophia was, indeed, like loving Sir Rich-
ard Steele's fair lady, "a liberal education;"
and Peter enjoyed the undivided benefit of her
rare talent for instruction.

He had been giving his attention to Astronomy of late, an unguarded remark of his
having betrayed to Sophia the extreme crudity

of his ideas respecting that science, and she had insisted upon his getting a popular primer, with diagrams, and mastering it as a preliminary to deeper study.

One evening he was in the smaller room of the two that, divided by an arch, served for study and drawing-room combined; and he was busily engaged in working out a simple practical illustration, by the aid of one of the aforesaid diagrams. The experiment required a lamp, a ball of cotton, and an orange transfixed by a knitting-needle, and it had something to do with the succession of the seasons, solar and lunar eclipses, and the varying lengths of day and night on different portions of our globe, though he was not very clear what.

" Don't you find you understand the inclination of the moon's orbit to the plane of the ecliptic better now?" said Sophia, as she came through the arch.

" I think I shall, as soon as I can get the moon to keep steadier," he said, with more hope than he felt; "and it's rather hard to remember whereabouts I am supposed to be on this orange."

" I must get you something to make that

clearer," she said; "and you haven't tilted the orange nearly enough. But leave it for a moment; I've brought you in this packet of letters and things the people at your old rooms have just sent down. I wish, while I am away—I shall be back in a minute—you would just run over them, and tell me if there are any papers you want kept, or if they may all be burned."

While she was gone, he undid the string which fastened the packet, and found, at the bottom of a mass of bills and documents of no value, the small oblong cheque-book which he had vowed never to see again. Somehow, as his eyes rested on its green cover, the old longing came upon him for a complete change of air and scene. He felt as if he *must* get away from that orange: there were no lamps but electric lights, and no oranges, on board the *Boomerang*.

But then, his last visit had not turned out a success: what if he were to find he had drawn another quarter of an hour with that irate matron of the music-room?

However, he had left her, as he remembered, in a comparatively pacific mood. She under-

6

stood him better now; and besides, thanks to the highly erratic system (if there was any system) on which the payments were made, the chances were immensely against his coming across the same old lady twice running. He thought he would risk that.

It was much more likely that he would meet Miss Tyrrell or Miss Davenport, or it might even be another person to whom he was unconsciously allied by the bond of dear friendship. The only question was, how far he could trust himself in such companionship. But here he felt himself guilty of a self-distrust that was unworthy of him. If, on the two previous occasions, he could not call to mind that he had entertained any deeper sentiment for either young lady than a cordial and sympathetic interest, was it likely that, now he was a married man, he would be more susceptible? He was as devoted to his Sophia as ever, but the wear and tear of several successive evenings spent in elementary Astronomy were telling upon his constitution. Such high thinking did not agree with him; he wanted a plainer mental diet for a change. Fifteen minutes spent in the society of some one with a mind rather less cultivated than his wife's would be very restful. Then, when he came back, he would give his whole mind to the orange again.

In short, all Peter's good resolutions were thrown overboard once more, and he wrote out a cheque for the usual amount in desperate fear lest Sophia might return before he could get it honored. He felt a certain compunction, even then, in presenting it to the severe and intensely respectable black marble timepiece which recorded the flying hours of his domestic bliss. He almost doubted whether it would countenance so irregular a proceeding; but, although it was on the verge of striking nine, it cashed the cheque without hesitation. . . .

It was midday : Peter was sitting on a folding seat, protected from the scorching sun by the awning which was stretched above and along the exposed side of the deck; and, to his great satisfaction, he found Miss Tyrrell reclining in a deck chair between himself and the railing, and a pleasant picture of fresh and graceful girlhood she presented.

As usual, he was not in time for the beginning of the conversation, for she was evidently commenting upon something he had said.

" How delightful it sounds," she was saying, "and what a free, unfettered kind of life yours must be, Mr. Tourmalin, from your description ! "

Now, this was awkward ; because he must have been giving her an airy description of his existence as the bachelor and butterfly he had ceased to be. He answered guardedly, awaiting his opportunity to lead up to a disclosure of the change in his circumstances since they had last met.

" It is pleasant enough," he said. " A little dull at times, perhaps," he added, thinking of the orange.

She laughed.

" Oh, you mustn't expect me to pity you !" she said. " I don't believe you need ever be dull, unless you choose. There must always be friends who are glad to see you."

" I am glad to think," said Peter, " that, when I do feel dull, I have at least one friend —one dear friend—from whom I may count upon a welcome ! "

He accompanied this speech with such a

look, that she could not well pretend to mistake his meaning ; and the next moment he regretted it, for he saw he had gone too far.

"That is a very pretty speech," she said, with a faint flush ; "but isn't it a little premature, Mr. Tourmalin, considering that we have scarcely known one another two days ! "

For the moment, Peter had forgotten the want of consecutiveness in these eccentric Time-Cheques. This interview should by rights have preceded the first he had had with her. He felt annoyed with himself, and still more with the unbusiness-like behavior of the Bank.

"I—I was anticipating, perhaps," he said. "But I assure you that we shall certainly *be* friends—I may even go so far as to say, dear friends—sooner or later. You see if I am not right ! "

Miss Tyrrell smiled.

"Are you sure," she said, with her eyes demurely lowered—are you sure that there is nobody who might object to our being on quite such intimate terms as that ? "

Peter started. Could she possibly have guessed, and how much did she know ?

"There could be nothing for anybody to object to," he said. "Are you—er—referring to any person in particular?"

She still kept her eyes down, but then she was occupied just at the moment in removing a loose splinter of bamboo from the arm of her chair.

"You mustn't think me curious or—or indiscreet, if I tell you," she said; "but before I knew you to speak to, I—I couldn't help noticing how often, as you sat on deck, you used to pull something out of your pocket and look at it."

"My watch?" suggested Peter, feeling uncomfortable.

"No, not your watch; it looked more like —well, like a photograph."

"It may have been a photograph, now you mention it," he admitted. "Well, Miss Tyrrell?"

"Well," she said, "I often amuse myself by making up stories about people I meet— quite strangers, I mean. And, do you know, I made up my mind that that photograph was the portrait of some one—some lady you are engaged to. I should so much like to know if I was right or not?"

Here was Peter's opportunity of revealing his real status, and preventing all chance of future misunderstanding. It was not too late; but still it might be best and kindest to break the news gradually.

"You were partly right and partly wrong," he said: "that was the portrait of a lady I was—er—*once* engaged to."

Unless Peter was very much mistaken, there was a new light in her face, an added bright. ness in her soft gray eyes as she raised them for an instant before resuming her labors upon the wicker-chair.

"Then you mean," she said softly, "that the engagement is broken off?"

Peter began to recognize that explanation was a less simple affair than it had seemed. If he said that he was no longer engaged but *married* to the original of that photograph, she would naturally want to know why he had just led her to believe, as he must have done, that he was still a careless and unattached bachelor; she would ask *when* and *where* he was married; and how could he give a straightforward and satisfactory answer to such questions?

And then another side of the case struck him. As a matter of fact he was undeniably married; but would he be strictly correct in describing himself as being so *in this particular interview?* It belonged properly to the time he had made the voyage home, and he was certainly not married *then.*

In the difficulty he was in he thought it best to go on telling the truth until it became absolutely impossible, and then fall back on invention.

"The fact is, Miss Tyrrell," he said, "that I can't be absolutely certain whether the engagement is ended or not at this precise moment."

Her face was alive with the sweetest sympathy.

"Poor Mr. Tourmalin!" she said, "how horribly anxious you must be to get back and know!"

"Ah!" said Peter, "yes, I—I shall know when I get home, I suppose."

And he sighed; for the orange recurred once more to his reluctant memory.

"Don't tell me if it pains you too much," she said gently. "I only ask because I do feel so sorry for you. Do you think that, when you do get home, you will find her married ? "

" I have every reason for believing so," he said.

" That will be a terrible blow for you, of course ? "

" A blow ? " said Peter, forgetting himself. " Good gracious me, no ! Why *should* it be ? I—I mean, I shall be prepared for it, don't you know ? "

" Then it's not so bad, after all ? " she said.

" It's not at all bad ! " said Peter, with a vague intention of loyalty to Sophia. " I like it ! "

" I think I understand," she said slowly : " you will not be sorry to find she has married ; but she may tell you that she never had the least intention of letting you go so easily ? "

" Yes," said Peter, " she may tell me that, certainly—(" if she finds out where I've been," he added, mentally.)

" And," she continued, " what would you do then ? "

" I suppose," he said—" I suppose I should have to do whatever she wished."

" Yes ! " she agreed warmly, " you *will* do

that, even if it costs you something, won't you? Because it will be the only right, the only honorable course to take—you will be the happier for it in the end, Mr. Tourmalin, I am sure you will!"

After all, it seemed to him that she must understand about the Time Cheques—or, why should she urge him to give them up if Sophia demanded such a sacrifice?

"No, I shall not," he said; "I shall miss these times terribly. You don't know what they are to me, or you wouldn't speak like that!"

"Mr. Tourmalin!" she cried, "I—I must not listen to you! You can't possibly mean what you seem to mean. It is wrong—wrong to me, and wrong to her—to say things that—that, for all you know, you are not free to say! Don't let me think badly of you!"

Peter was absolutely horrified! What had he said to agitate her like that? He had merely meant to express the pleasure he found in these brief and stolen visits to the *Boomerang;* and she had misconstrued him like this! At all hazards, he must explain now, if it took him days to make it clear.

"My dear Miss Tyrrell," he protested earnestly, "you quite misunderstood me—you did indeed! Pray be calm, and I will endeavor to make my position a little clearer than I'm afraid I have done. The worst of it is," he added, "that the whole thing has got into such a muddle that, for the life of me, I can't exactly make out what my position is at the present moment!"

"You can if you will only recollect that you are this mourning-pin," said a familiar voice; and, with the abruptness characteristic of the Time Cheque system, he was back in his study, staring at the ground glass globe of the lamp and the transfixed orange. The clock behind him was striking nine, and Sophia was offering him a pin with a big black head.

"Oh! am I the mourning-pin?" he repeated, helplessly.

"Really, Peter," said Sophia, "I think the pin just at this moment, has the more intelligent expression of the two. Do try to look a little less idiotic! Now, see; you stick the pin into the orange to represent your point of view, and then keep on twirling it slowly round."

So Peter twirled the orange slowly round for the remainder of the evening, though his thoughts were far away with Miss Tyrrell. He was wondering what she could have thought of him, and, worse still, what she would think if she could see him as he was employed at that moment?

"I tell you what we must do, Peter—when you get a little more advanced," said Sophia, enthusiastically, that evening, "we must see if we can't pick up a small second-hand orrery somewhere—it would be so nice to have one!"

"Oh, delightful!" he said absently.

He was not very clear as to what an orrery was, unless it was the dusty machine that was worked with handles at sundry Assembly-room lectures he had attended in early youth. But of one thing he felt grimly certain—that it was something which would render it necessary to draw more Time Cheques!

CHAPTER V.

*A Series of Cheques: their Advantages and Drawbacks.
—An Unknown Factor.—Uncompleted Confidences.—
Ibsen, with Intervals.—A Disappointment.—A "Search
Question" from Sophia.—Confidence restored.*

WHETHER it was natural sin on Peter's part,
or an excusable spirit of revolt against the op-
pression of an orrery which Sophia succeeded
in picking up a great bargain at an auction
somewhere, his drafts on the Anglo-Australian Time Bank did not end with the one recorded in the preceding chapter.

And, which was more discreditable still, he
no longer pretended to himself that he meant
to stop until his balance was completely exhausted. His only care now was to economize,
to regulate his expenditure by spreading his
drawings over as long a period as possi-

ble. With this object he made a careful
calculation, and found there were still several hours to his credit; whereupon, lest he
should yield to the temptation of drawing
too much at any one time, he made out a number of cheques for fifteen minutes apiece, and
limited himself to one a week—an allowance
which, even under the severest provocation,
he rarely permitted himself to exceed.

These weekly excursions, short as they were,
were a source of the greatest comfort to him,
especially now that he had thrown off any idea
of moral responsibility.

By degrees he possessed himself of most of
the back-numbers, if they may be so termed,
of his dual romance. At one time, he found
himself being presented by the grateful Sir
William to his daughter; and now that he
knew what service he had rendered the Judge,
he was less at sea than he would certainly have
been otherwise. Another time, he discovered
himself in the act of dragging Miss Davenport
unceremoniously back from the bulwarks; but
here again his memory furnished him with the
proper excuse for conduct which, considering
that he was not supposed to be acquainted with

her, he might have found it difficult to account for satisfactorily. So, after all, there did seem to be a sort of method in the operation of the Time Cheques, arbitrary as it appeared.

One fact that went far to reconcile him to his own conscience was the circumstance that, though the relations he stood in toward both young ladies varied at each interview with the most bewildering uncertainty, so that one week he would be upon the closest and most confidential terms, and the next be thrown back into the conventional formality of a first introduction—these relations never again approached the dangerous level of sentiment which had so alarmed him.

He flattered himself that the judicious attitude he was adopting to both was correcting the false impressions which might have—and for that matter actually had—been given.

He was always pleased to see them again, whichever one it was ; they were simply charming friends—frank, natural, unaffected girls—and not too clever. Sometimes, indeed, he recognized, and did his best to discourage, symptoms of a dawning tenderness on their part which it was not in his power to reciprocate.

Peter was in no danger of losing his heart to either; possibly the attractions of each served as a conductor to protect him from the influence of the other. He enjoyed their society, their evident appreciation of all he said and did, but that was all; and as they recognized that there could be no closer bond than that of cordial friendship between them, he was relieved of all misgivings.

Surely it was a blameless and legitimate manner, even for a married man, of spending the idle moments which belonged properly to the days of his bachelorhood! Still, he did not confide this harmless secret of his to Sophia; he might tell her when it was all over, but not so long as her disapproval could affect his plans. And he had an instinct that such a story as he had to tell would fail to appeal to a person of her accurately logical habit of mind.

So, on one occasion when he discovered that he had lost one of the loose cheques he now carried constantly about with him, it was with a feeling very like panic that he reflected that he might have dropped it about the house, where its unusual form would inevitably provoke Sophia's curiosity ; and he was much re-assured when he was able to conclude, from the fact that she made no reference to it, that he must have lost it out of doors.

It must have been some time after this before his serenity again met with a slight shock : he was walking up and down the deck with Miss Davenport—it happened to be one of the days when he knew her very well indeed.

"Sometimes," she was saying, " I feel as if I *must* speak to somebody ! "

" You know where you will always find a very willing listener ! " he said, with a kind of fatherly floweriness that he felt sat well upon him.

" I didn't mean you," she said—" to some girl of my own age, I meant."

" Oh ! " said Peter, " well, that's a very natural feeling, I'm sure. I can quite understand it ! "

" Then you wouldn't mind—you wouldn't be angry if I did ? " she said, looking up at him with her great childishly serious eyes.

" My dear child," said Peter, getting more fatherly every moment, " how could I possibly object to your speaking to any lady on board if you want to ? "

He would have liked to make one or two exceptions perhaps ; but he thought he had better not.

"I am so glad," she said, "because I did— this very morning. I did so want some one to advise me—to tell me what a girl ought to do, what she would do herself in my place."

"Ah!" said Peter, sympathetically, "it is— er—a difficult position for you, no doubt."

"And for you, too!" she said quickly ; "re- member that."

"And for me, *too*, of course," said Peter, as- senting, as he always did now from habit, to anything he did not understand at the mo- ment. "My position might be described as one of—er—difficulty, certainly. And so you asked advice about yours, eh?"

"I couldn't very well help myself," she said. "There was a girl, a little older than I am, per- haps, sitting next to me on deck, and she men- tioned your name, and somehow—I hardly know how it came about—but she seemed so kind, and so interested in it all, that—that I believe I told her everything. . . . You aren't *angry* with me, are you, Peter?"

She had been making a *confidante* of Miss

Tyrrell! It was awkward, extremely awkward and annoying, if, as he began to fear, her confidences were of a tender character.

"I—I am not exactly angry," he said; "but I do think you might be more careful whom you speak to. What did you tell her?"

"*All!*" she said, with the same little quiver in her underlip he had noticed before.

"That is no answer," said Peter (it certainly was none for him). "Tell me *what* you said?"

"I—I told her about you, and about me . . . and—and about *him!*"

"Oh!" said Peter, "about me, and you, and him? Well, and—and how did she *take* it?"

"She didn't say very much; she turned very pale. It was rather rough at the time, and I don't think she can be a very good sailor; for before I had even finished she got up and went below, and I haven't seen her since."

"But you told her about 'him'?" he persisted; "and when you say 'him,' I presume you refer to—"?

Here he paused expectantly.

"Of course!" she answered, with a touch of impatience. "Whom else should I be *likely* to refer to?"

"It's excessively absurd!" said Peter, driven
to candor at last. "I—I remember perfectly
that you did mention all the circumstances at
the time; but I've a shocking memory for
names, and, just for the minute, I—I find it
difficult to recall where 'he' comes in exactly.
Curious, isn't it?"

"Curious?" she said, passionately; "it's
abominable!"

"It is," agreed Peter; "I quite admit that
I *ought* to know—only, I *don't.*"

"This is cruel, unmanly!" she said, broken-
ly. "How *could* you forget—how can you
insult me by *pretending* that you could forget
such a thing as that? It is odious of you to
make a—a joke of it all, when you know perfectly well that—"

"My—my dear young lady!" he declared,
as she left her speech unfinished, "I am as far
from any disposition to be jocular as ever I
was in my life. Let me beg you to be a little
more explicit. We seem to have got into a
trifling misunderstanding, which, I am sure, a
little patience will easily put right." . . .

"Put right?" said Sophia, behind him.
"I was not aware, Peter, that the clock

was out of order. What is the matter with it ?"

He almost staggered back from the chimney-piece, upon which he had found himself leaning in an attitude of earnest persuasion.

"I—I was only thinking, my love," he said, "that it wanted regulating."

"If it does," said Sophia, "you are hardly the proper person to do it Peter. The less you meddle with it the better, I should think !"

"Perhaps so, my dear Sophia, perhaps so !" said Peter, sitting down with the utmost docility.

He had narrowly escaped exciting suspicion. It was fortunate that there was nothing compromising in the few words she had overheard, but he must not allow himself to be caught so near the clock again.

He was not a little disturbed by the tenor of this last interview. It was bad enough that in some way he seemed to have seriously displeased Miss Davenport; but, besides that, he could not contemplate without uneasiness the probable effect which her confidences, whatever their exact purport, might have upon

Miss Tyrrell. For hitherto he had seen no necessity to mention to one young lady that he was even distantly acquainted with the other. As he never by any chance drew them both together, there seemed no object in volunteering such information.

But this only made him more apprehensive of a scene when his next turn with Miss Tyrrell arrived. Perhaps, he thought, it would be wiser to keep away from the *Boomerang* for a week or two, and give them all time to calm down a little.

However, he had the moral, or rather the immoral, courage to present a check as usual at the end of the next week, with results that were even less in accordance with his anticipations than before.

It came about in this way. He was comfortably seated by the fireplace opposite Sophia in a cosy, domesticated fashion, and was reading to her aloud; for he had been let off the orrery that evening. The book he was reading by Sophia's particular request was Ibsen's *Doll's House,* and it was not the fault of the subject (which interested her deeply), but of Peter's elocution, which was poor, that, on

glancing from the text, he found that she
had sunk into a profound and peaceful slum-
ber.

It was a chance he had been waiting for all
day. He was rather tired of Nora, with her
innocence and her macaroons, her tarantella
and her taradiddles, her forgery and her fancy
dress, and he had the cheque by him in readiness; so he stole on tiptoe to the mantelpiece,
slipped the paper under the clock, and was just
in time to sink back into his easy-chair before
it turned out to be one of the revolving-seats
in the dining-saloon on the *Boomerang*.

There was a tumbler of whisky-and-seltzer
on the table in front of him, and he was sitting
in close confabulation with his former acquaintance, Mr. Perkins, the bank manager.

"That's precisely what I don't know, sir,
and what I'm determined to find out!" were
the first words he heard from the latter gentleman, who looked flushed and angry. "But
it's a scandalous thing, isn't it?"

"Very," said Peter, rather bored and deeply
disappointed; for the manager was but an indifferent substitute for the companion he had
been counting upon. "Oh, very!"

"Have you happened to hear anything said about it yourself?" inquired his friend.

"Not a word!" said Peter, with the veracity he always endeavored to maintain on these occasions.

"To go and shift a statement of that kind on to my shoulders like that, it's like the fellow's confounded impudence!"

For the moment Peter felt a twinge; could the other be referring to anything he had said himself in the music-room? But the manager was evidently not angry with *him*, so it must be some other fellow. Only Peter decided not to allude to the faulty working of the time cheques, as he had half intended to do. Perkins was not in the mood for remonstrances just then.

"Most impudent, I must say," he replied. "By the way," he added carelessly, "what was the statement exactly?"

"Why, God bless my soul, sir!" cried the manager, with unnecessary vehemence, "haven't I been telling you the whole story? Didn't you just ask me who the fellow was who has brought me into this business?"

"So I did," said Peter, "and—and who *was* he?"

" Your attention seems very wandering this
evening! Why, I told you the old woman
wouldn't give me his name."

Peter's alarm returned at this allusion to an
old woman; what old woman could it be but
the terrible matron whom he had encountered
in the music-room? However, it was fortunate
that she had not mentioned any names; if Perkins knew that he had put all the blame of his
entanglements upon the manager's broad shoulders, he would certainly consider it an ungrate-
ful return for what was intended as a kindness.

" So you said before," he remarked; "some
old women are so obstinate!"

" Obstinate? That's the first sensible remark
you've made for a long while!" said his candid
friend. " I should think she was obstinate!
Why, I talked myself hoarse trying to make
that old harridan believe that I was as innocent
as an unborn babe of any responsibility for this
precious scandal—that I'd never so much as
heard it breathed till she told me of it; but it
wasn't any good, sir; she would have it that I
was the originator!"

(" So you were!" thought Peter, though he
prudently refrained from saying so.)

"She's going to kick up the dooce's own delight as soon as she meets her brother; and all I could get her to say was that then, and not till then, she would give me an opportunity of having it out with the cowardly villain, whoever he may be, that has dared to lay all this gossip at *my* door!"

Peter did not quarrel with this arrangement of the old lady's, for he would certainly not be on board the *Boomerang* when she arrived at Plymouth.

"Ah!" he said, with as much interest as he could display in a subject that did not concern him, "he'll find that unpleasant, I dare say."

"I think he will!" said Mr. Perkins, emphatically. "Unless he retracts his infamous calumny. I—I'll kick him from one end of the ship to the other!"

Involuntarily Peter's eyes sought his friend's boots, which, as he sat in a corner seat with his feet extended, were much in evidence; they were strong, suitable boots, stouter than those generally worn on a sea-voyage, and Peter could not repress a slight shudder.

"From one end of the ship to the other,"

he repeated ; " that—that's rather a long
way ! "

" Quite long enough for him, though not
nearly long enough for me ! " said the Manager. " I'll teach him to mix me up in these
squabbles, when I find him, sir—when I find
him ! Here, steward, bring some more of
these dry biscuits ; you'll have some more,
won't you ? "

But Peter was not in the vein for dry
biscuits at that moment, and the Manager continued :

" By-the-by, *you* might help me in this if
you only will. I want to find out if I can
before we reach Gib, who this fellow is, but
the less I talk about the affair the better."

" Oh ! yes," said Peter. " I—I wouldn't
talk about it at all, if I were you."

" No. I dare say you're right — can't be
too careful with an old cat like that. Well,
what I want you to do is to try and find out
—quietly, you know—who this infernal fellow
is ! "

" Well, I dare say I could do that," said
Peter.

" No one would think a mild, innocent-

looking little chap like you had any particular
motive for asking: you might ask some of
the men in the smoking-room, and pick up
some clew or other."

"So I might," said Peter,—"good idea!"

"Or, I'll tell you what—you might pump
the old lady for me, eh?"

"I don't think I quite care about pumping
the old lady," said Peter, "but anything else
I'll do with pleasure."

"Thanks," said the Manager, "that's a
good fellow. I knew I could depend upon
you!"

"You can," replied Peter, "though, I
fancy," he added, soothingly—"indeed, I am
sure you will find that the old woman has
made a good deal out of nothing at all." . . .

"*What* old woman, Peter?" asked Sophia
whith drowsy asperity. "Not Mrs. Linden,
surely!"

Mrs. Linden! Was that the name of the
old she-dragon of the music-room? Why, of
course not; he was in his arm-chair by his
own fire, reading Ibsen to his wife!

"I don't know, indeed, my love—it *may*
be Mrs. Linden," he answered cautiously.

"Nonsense!" said Sophia, crossly. "She's not meant to be old in the play, and *who* says 'the old woman has made a good deal out of nothing?' Helmer, or Doctor Rank, or Krogstad, or who? You do read so badly, it's quite impossible to make out!"

"*No* one says it, my dear Sophia; at least, it's not in my edition of the text. You—you must have imagined it, I think!"

"I certainly thought I heard you read it out," she replied; "but your voice is so monotonous, that it's just possible I dropped off for a minute or two."

"I dropped off myself about the same time," he confessed hypocritically.

"You wouldn't drop off, or allow me to drop off either, Peter," said Sophia, who was now thoroughly awake again, "if you felt a more intelligent interest in the tremendous problem Ibsen has set in this play. I don't believe you realize in the least what the lesson is that he means to teach; now *do* you, Peter?"

"Well, I'm not sure that I do altogether, my love," he admitted.

"I thought as much! What Ibsen insists

upon is, the absolute necessity of one-ness between man and wife, Peter. They must belong
to each other, complete each other—they must
be Twin Souls. Are *you* a Twin Soul, Peter?"

"Upon my word, my dear, I can't say!" he
replied, in some perplexity. In the present
very divided state of his sympathies, he could
not help thinking that his Soul was more like
a Triplet.

"But think," persisted Sophia, earnestly:
"have you shared all your Past with me? Is
there nothing you have kept back—no feelings, no experiences, which you confine to
your own bosom? When you left me to take
that voyage, you promised that nothing should
induce you to be more than civil to any woman,
however young and attractive, with whom Fate
might bring you in contact. I want you to tell
me, Peter, whether, when you were returning
home on board the *Boomerang,* you kept that
promise or not?"

Fortunately for him, she put her question
in a form which made it easy to give a satisfactory and a truthful answer.

"When I was returning home on board the
Boomerang," he said, "I did not, to the best of

my recollection and belief, exchange two words
with any female whatever, attractive or otherwise—until," he added, with a timely recollection that she had come on board at Gibraltar—
"until I met you. You pain me with these
suspicions, Sophia—you do, indeed!"

"I believe you, Peter," she said, moved by
his sincerity, which, paradoxical as it may
sound, was quite real; for his intentions had
been so excellent throughout, that he felt injured by her doubts. "You have never told
me a falsehood yet; but for some time I have
been tormented by a fancy that you were con-
cealing something from me. I can hardly say
what gave me such an impression—a glance,
a tone, trifles which, I am glad to think now,
had not the importance I invested them with.
Ah, Peter, never treat me as Helmer did Nora!
Never shut me out from the serious side of
your life, and think to make amends by calling
me your 'little lark,' or your 'squirrel;' you
must not look upon me as a mere doll!"

"My *dear* Sophia!" he exclaimed, "I should
never think of addressing you as either a squirrel
or a lark; and any one less like a doll in every
respect I never met!"

"I hope you will always think so, Peter," she said; "for I tell you frankly, that if I once discovered that you had ceased to trust me, that you lived in a world apart into which I was not admitted, that very moment, Peter, I should act just as Nora did—I should leave you; for our marriage would have ceased to be one in any true sense of the word!"

The mere idea of being abandoned by Sophia made him shiver. What a risk he had been running, after all! Was it worth while to peril his domestic happiness for the sake of a few more conversations with two young ladies, whose remarks were mostly enigmatic, and for whom he was conscious in his heart of hearts of not caring two straws?

"Sophia," he said plaintively, "don't talk of leaving me! What should I do without you? Who would teach me Astronomy and things? You *know* I don't care for anybody but you! Why will you dwell on such unpleasant subjects?"

"I was wrong, Peter," she confessed—"indeed, I doubt you no longer. It was all my morbid imagination that led me to do you such injustice. Forgive me, and let us say no more about it!"

"I do forgive you," was his generous reply to this appeal, which, coming from Sophia, was a very handsome apology, "and we *will* say no more about it."

And, upon the whole, Peter thought he had got out of a particularly tight place with more credit than he had any reason to expect—a conclusion in which the reader, however much he or she may disapprove of his conduct on moral grounds, will probably be inclined to agree with him.

CHAPTER VI.

FOIL AND COUNTERFOIL.

The Duties of Authorship.—Peter's Continued Perversity and its Unforeseen Results.—"Alfred."—The Tragic Note.—An Interrupted Crisis.—A Domestic Surprise.

It would be more satisfactory to an author's feelings, especially when he is aware that he will be held accountable by an indignant public for the slightest deviation on his hero's part from the narrow path of ideal rectitude—it would be more satisfactory to be able to record that this latest warning had a permanent effect upon Peter Tourmalin's rather shifty disposition.

But an author, even of a modest performance such as this, can not but feel himself in a position of grave responsibility. He must relate such facts as he has been able to collect, without suppression on the one side or distortion on the other. It is a duty he can not and dare not evade, under penalty of forfeiting the confidence of his readers.

Peter Tourmalin *did* draw more Time Cheques, he *did* go back to the *Boomerang*, and it would be useless to assert the contrary. We may be able to rehabilitate him to some extent before this story concludes; at present, we can only follow his career with pain and disapproval.

Some allowances must be made for the peculiar nature of the case. To a person of Peter's natural inclination to the study of psychology, there was a strong fascination in watching the gradual unfolding and revelation of two characters so opposite and so interesting as those of Miss Tyrrell and Miss Davenport. That was the point of view he took himself, and it is difficult to say that such a plea is wholly without plausibility.

Then, too, he was intensely curious to know how it would all end, and he might ascertain that in the very next quarter of an hour he drew; there was absolutely no telling.

As for Sophia's threat, that soon lost all terrors for him. She would abandon him, no doubt, if she ever knew; but who was going to tell her, and how could she possibly discover the truth unaided, especially now that her awakening suspicions had been lulled? His secret was perfectly safe, and he could unravel the tangled thread of the history of his remaining extra hours on board the *Boomerang* without any other hindrance than that of his own scruples—which practically amounted to no hindrance at all.

So Peter continued to be the slave of his clock and his cheque-book, from the counterfoils of which he was disagreeably surprised to discover that he had drawn more frequently, and in consequence had an even smaller balance left to his credit than he had supposed.

However, he consoled himself by concluding that one or two cheques had probably been mislaid, and were still unpresented, while he was entitled to some additional time in respect of compound interest; so that he need not stint himself at present. Fifteen minutes a week was not an extravagant allowance; and sooner or later, even with the utmost economy, a day would come when his balance would be exhausted, and his cheques returned from the clock marked "No effects—refer to drawer," or some equivalent intimation.

But that day was still distant, and in the mean time he went on drawing with a light heart.

It was a Saturday evening, the day on which Peter generally presented his weekly cheque; but, although it was nearly half-past ten, he had had no opportunity of doing so as yet. He was in the drawing-room, and Sophia was reading aloud to him this time, an article on "Bi-metalism" from one of the reviews; for she had been an ardent bi-metalist from early girlhood, and she naturally wished to win Peter from his Laodicean apathy on so momentous a subject. He listened with surface resignation, although inwardly he was in a fever of impatience to get back upon the *Boomerang*, where Miss Davenport had been more interesting than usual on his last visit. But he could hardly rise and slip a cheque under the clock before Sophia's very eyes without inventing some decent pretext for such an action, and bi-metalism had reduced him to a mental condition which was no longer fertile in expedients.

Suddenly Sophia stopped reading and remarked:

"If I remember right, Professor Dibbs has stated the argument more correctly in his little book on *Currency*. It would be interesting to compare the two; I'll get it."

As Professor Dibbs's work was apparently on a shelf in the study, Sophia took the lamp into the further room.

"Now's my time!" thought Peter, as he brought out the cheque from his waistcoat-pocket. "I mayn't get such another chance this evening."

Even if Sophia could lay her hand on the volume at once, he would have had his quarter of an hour and be comfortably back long before she could pass the arch which separated the two rooms; for, as we have seen, this instantaneous action was one of the chief recommendations of the Time Cheques.

So he cashed his cheque, and was at once transported to the secluded passage between the deck-cabins, the identical place where he had first conversed with Miss Davenport. He was on the same steamer-chair, too, and she was at his side; the wind carried the faint strains of a set of "Lancers" to them; from all of which circumstances he drew the infer-

ence that he was going to be favored with the
sequel to the conversation that had been so
incongruously broken in upon by Sophia's
question respecting the comparative merits of
bottle-jacks in the Tottenham Court Road
warehouse. This was so far satisfactory, indicating as it did that he was at last, after
so much trying back, to make some real
progress.

" What I want to know first," Miss Davenport was saying, " is whether you are capable
of facing danger for my sake ? "

" I thought," he remonstrated mildly, " that
I had already given proof of that ! "

" The danger you faced then threatened
only me. But, supposing you had to meet a
danger to yourself, could you be firm and
cool ? Much will depend on that."

" I—I think," he answered frankly, " that
perhaps you had better not count upon me.
I have never been a man to court danger ; it
might find me equal to it if it came—or it
might not."

He did not mean to give it the opportunity.

" Then we are lost, that is all ! " she said,

with gloomy conviction.   "Lost, both of
us!"

Peter certainly intended to be lost if the
moment of trial ever arrived. Even now he
was resolving, for about the twentieth time
that this positively should be his very last
cheque; for he by no means liked the manner in which the situation seemed to be de-
veloping.

But, seeing that the danger, whatever it
might be, was still far enough off, he thought,
very sensibly, that it would be a pity to cloud
this last interview by any confession of pusilla-
nimity. Knowing that he would return no
more, he could surely afford to treat with
contempt any consequences his imprudence
might have entailed.

So he laughed, as he said:

"You musn't conclude that I'm a coward
because I don't care to boast. On the contrary, I believe I am not exactly deficient in
physical courage."

"You are not?" she cried, relieved. "Then
—then you would not be afraid to face a desperate man?"

"Not a dozen desperate men, if it comes to

that!" said Peter, supported by the certainty
that it would not come to so much as half a
desperate man.

"Then I can tell you *now* what I have
scarcely dared to think of before. Peter, you
will have to reckon with Alfred!"

"Well, I'm not much alarmed at anything
Alfred may do!" said Peter, wondering who
the deuce Alfred was.

"He will come on board; he will demand
an explanation; he will insist on seeing you!"
she cried.

"*Let* him!" said Peter.

"You are brave—braver even than I thought;
but, ah! Peter, you don't know what Alfred
is!"

Peter did not even know who Alfred was,
but he was unmoved.

"You leave Alfred to me," he said, confi-
dently, "I'll settle *him!*"

"But I must tell you all. I—I led you to
believe that Alfred would raise no objections;
that he would quietly accept facts which it is
useless to contend against. He will do nothing
of the sort! He is a man of violent passions
—fierce and relentless when wronged. In the

first burst of fury at meeting you, when he comes on board, he is capable of some terrible vengeance, which nothing but perfect coolness on your part—perhaps not even that—will be able to avert. And I—I have brought this upon you!"

"Don't cry," said Peter. "You see, I'm perfectly calm. *I* don't mind it. If Alfred considers himself wronged by me—though, what I have ever done to give him any reason for revenging himself by personal violence, I must say I can't conceive—"

She stopped him.

"Ah! you have given him cause enough!" she cried. "What is the use of taking that tone to me?"

"I want to see Alfred's point of view, that's all," said Peter. "What does he complain of?"

"*What does he complain of?* You ask me that, when—Peter," she broke off suddenly, "there is somebody round the corner listening to us—a woman, I'm sure of it. I heard the rustle of a dress. . . . Go and see if there is not!"

Go and see, and find himself face to face

with Miss Tyrrell, who might faint or go into hysterics. Peter knew better than that.

"It's merely your fancy," he said, soothingly. "Who can be there? They are all at the other end of the ship, dancing. Go on telling me about Alfred. I don't yet understand how I have managed to offend him."

"Are you really so dull," she said, with a slight touch of temper, "that you can't see that a man who thought he was going to meet the woman he was engaged to, and finds she has learned to care for—for somebody else, is likely, even if he was the mildest man in the world—which Alfred is far from being—to betray some annoyance?"

"No, I see that," said Peter; "but—but he can't blame me. *I* couldn't help it!"

He said this, although her last speech had opened his eyes considerably. He knew now who Alfred was, and also that, in some moment of madness which was in one of the quarters of an hour he had not yet drawn, he must have placed himself in the position of Alfred's rival.

What was he to do? He could not, without brutality, tell this poor girl that he had not the smallest intention of depriving Alfred of her affections; it was better, and easier too, to humor her for the short time that remained.

" Alfred will not take that as an excuse," she said. " It is true we could neither of us help what has happened, but that will not alter the fact that he is quite capable of shooting us both the instant he comes on deck. Alfred is like that ! "

" Well," said Peter, unable to abstain from a little more of such very cheap heroism, " I do not fear death—with you ! "

" Say that once more," she said ; which Peter very obligingly did. " Oh, Peter, how I admire you now ! How little I knew you were capable of going so calmly to your doom ! You give me courage. I feel that I, too, can face death ; only not *that* death—it is so horrid to be shot ! "

" It would be unpleasant," said Peter, placidly, " but soon over."

" No," she said, " I couldn't bear it. I can see him pointing his revolver—for he always carries one, even at a picnic—first at *your* head, then mine ! No, Peter ; since we must die, I prefer at least to do so without bloodshed ! "

" So do I," he agreed, " very much."

" You do?" she cried. " Then, oh, Peter! why should we wait any longer for a fate that is inevitable? Let us do it now, together!"

" Do *what*?" said Peter.

" Slip over the side together; it would be quite easy, no one will see us. Let us plunge arm-in-arm into the merciful sea! A little struggle—a moment's battle for breath—then all will be over!"

" Yes, I suppose it *would* be over then"; he said; " but we should have to swallow such a lot of salt water first!"

He reflected that, even if he emerged from the agonies of drowning, to find himself bi-metalizing with Sophia, the experience would be none the less unpleasant while it lasted. There really must be some limit to his complaisance, and he set it at suicide.

" No," he said; " I have always held that to escape a difficulty by putting an end to one's own life is a cowardly proceeding."

" I *am* a coward," she said; " but oh, Peter, be a coward with me for once!"

" Ask me anything else!" he said firmly, but not stoop to cowardice. There is really

no necessity for it, you see," he added, feeling
that he had better speak out plainly. "I have
no doubt that Alfred will listen to reason ; and
when he is told that, although, as is excusable
enough with two natures that have much in
common, we—we have found a mutual pleasure in each other's society—there has been
nothing on either side inconsistent with the—
the most ordinary friendship; when he hears
that . . . Where are you going?" for she was
rising from her chair.

"Where am I going?" she replied, with an
unsteady laugh. "Why, overboard, if you
care to know!"

"But you mustn't!" he cried, scarcely knowing what he said. "The—the captain wouldn't
like it. There's a penalty, I'm sure, for leaving the ship while it's in motion—I've seen it
on a notice!"

"There is a penalty for having believed in
you," she replied bitterly, "and I am going to
pay it!"

She broke away and rushed out upon the
deck into the starlight, with Peter in pursuit.
Here was a nice result of his philandering, he
thought bitterly. And yet, what had he done?

How could he help the consequences of follies committed in time he had not even spent yet? However, what he had to do now was to prevent Miss Davenport from leaping overboard at any cost. He would even promise to jump over with her, if that would soothe her, and of course he could appoint some time next day— say, after breakfast for the performance.

He ran down the shadowy deck until he overtook a flying female form, whose hand he seized as she crouched against the bulwarks.

"Miss Davenport, if you will only just . . . " he began, when, without warning, he found himself back upon his own hearth-rug, holding Sophia firmly by the wrist!

He felt confused, as well he might, but he tried to pass it off.

" Did you find *Dibbs on Currency*, my dear?" he inquired, with a ghastly smile, as he dropped her hand.

" I did not," said Sophia, gravely; " I was otherwise engaged. Peter, what have you been doing?"

"What have I been doing?" he said. " Why, it's not a minute since you went into the study to get that book; look at the clock and see!"

"Don't appeal to the clock, Peter—answer my question. How have you been occupied?"

"I've been waiting for you to finish that article on bi-metalism," he had the hardihood to say. "Deuced well-written article it is, too; so clear!"

"I don't refer to what you were doing here," said Sophia. "What were you doing on board the *Boomerang?*"

"It—it's so long ago that I really forget," he said. "I—I read Buckle on deck, and I talked with a man named Perkins—nice fellow he was—manager of a bank out in Australia."

"It's useless to prevaricate, Peter!" she said. "What I want to know is, who was that girl, and why should she attempt to destroy herself?"

He could hardly believe his ears.

"Girl!" he stammered. "How do you know that any girl attempted anything of that sort?"

"How do I know, Peter?" said Sophia. "I will tell you how I know. *I was on board the Boomerang too!*"

At this awful piece of intelligence, Peter dropped into his arm-chair, speechless and quaking. What would come next he could not tell; but anything seemed possible, and even probable, after that!

9

CHAPTER VII.

THE CULMINATING CHEQUE.

Sophia gives an Explanation and Requests one.—Her Verdict.—Peter Overruled.

"BEFORE I say anything else," said Sophia, who was still standing upon the hearth-rug, gazing down upon the wretched Peter as he sat huddled up in his chair, "you would probably like to know how I came to follow you to that ship. It is a long story, but I will tell you if you wish to hear?"

Peter's lips moved without producing any articulate sounds, and Sophia proceeded:

"Some weeks ago," she said, "one afternoon when you had gone out for a walk, I found what seemed to be a loose cheque on the carpet. I knew how carelessly you leave things about, and I picked it up and found that, though it was like a cheque in other respects, it was rather curiously worded. I could not understand it at all, but it seemed to have something to do with the ship you came home from Australia in; so, intending to ask you for an explanation when you came in, I thought in the mean time I would put it in some safe place where I should be sure to see it, and I put it behind the clock; and then—oh, Peter!—"

Peter understood. The cheques were all payable to "self or bearer." Sophia had innocently presented one, and it had been paid. If he had only taken "order" cheques, this would not have happened, but it was too late now! He continued to imitate the tactics of that eminent strategist, Brer Rabbit; in other words, he "lay low and said nuffin," while Sophia continued:

"Then, without in the least knowing how I came there, I found I was on a big steamer, and as I walked along, perfectly bewildered, I saw the name *Boomerang* painted on some fire-buckets, and of course I knew then that that was your ship. I fancied that perhaps, in some way, you might be on board too, and would explain how this had happened to me. At all events, I decided to find out if you were;

and, seeing a girl reading on deck, I took a chair near her, and after a few introductory remarks I mentioned your name. The effect upon her was such as to convince me that she felt more than an ordinary interest in you. By degrees I drew from her the whole story of her relations with you: she even asked me—*me*—for advice!"

So Miss Davenport's *confidante* had not been Miss Tyrrell after all—but Sophia! If he had only known that before!

"I could not speak to her," continued Sophia, "I felt stifled, stupefied by what I had heard! I could bear no more; and so I rose and left her, and walked down some stairs, and somehow found myself back in our own room again! I was more bewildered than ever. I looked for the cheque, but there was nothing, and soon I was forced to believe that the whole thing was imaginary. Still, I was not wholly satisfied. You may remember how I questioned you one evening when you were reading the *Doll's House* to me; well, your answers quite reassured me for the time. I told myself that my suspicions were too wildly improbable not to have been a delusion.

I was even afraid that my brain must be slightly affected, for I had always prided myself upon having my imagination under thorough control. But by degrees, Peter—by degrees I began to doubt again whether it was really nothing but fancy on my part. I noticed that your manner was suspiciously odd at times. I discovered that there was one drawer in your secretary that you kept carefully locked. I caught your eye wandering toward the clock from time to time. *What* I suspected I hardly know; but I felt certain that I should find the explanation of that mystery in the locked drawer. I tried key after key, until I found one that fitted. Oh, I am not at all ashamed of it! Had I not a *right* to know? There were no letters, nothing but a cheque-book; but that cheque-book proved to me that, after all, I had imagined nothing: all the cheques were the same as the one I found on the carpet! I tore one out and kept it by me, and from that time I watched you closely. I saw how restless and impatient you were this evening, and I was certain that you were intending to use a cheque from that book. You were bent on getting

back to the *Boomerang*, and I was equally
determined that, if I could help it, you
should not go alone. Only I could not be
quite sure how you managed to get there, and
at last I hit upon a little device for finding
out. There is no such person as Professor
Dibbs, Peter; I invented him to put you off
your guard. As I passed into the other room
with the lamp, I saw you, reflected in the mir-
ror over the study chimneypiece, rise and go
to the drawing-room mantelpiece: you had a
slip of paper in your hand—a cheque, of
course. I had the cheque I tore out hidden
in the waistband of my dress; and so, as soon
as I saw you slip your cheque behind the clock
in the drawing-room, I put *my* cheque behind
the one in the study. I was on the deck at
once, and it was dark, but I could hear your
voice and another's—round a corner. I held
my breath and listened. What I heard, you
know!"

Peter shrank up in his chair, utterly confounded by this last vagary on the part of the
Time Cheques. He certainly would not have
supposed that the mere presentation even of a
" bearer " cheque by Sophia would entitle her

to the same fifteen minutes he was receiving himself. He could only account for it by the fact that the two cheques were cashed simultaneously at two separate clocks; but even this explanation was not wholly satisfactory.

He found his voice at last:

"Well," he said, "now that you know all, what are you going to do about it, Sophia? I —would rather know the worst!"

"I will tell you that in good time," she replied; "but, first of all, I want you to tell me exactly how you came to have these cheques, and what use you made of them on previous occasions?"

So, slightly reassured by her manner, which was composed, Peter gave her a plain, unvarnished account of the way in which he had been led to deposit his extra time, and the whole story of his interviews with Miss Davenport. He did not mention any others, because he felt that the affair was quite complicated enough without dragging in extraneous and irrelevant matter.

"I may have been imprudent," he concluded; "but I do assure you, Sophia, that in all the quarters of an hour I have had as yet,

I never once behaved to that young lady in any capacity but that of a friend. I only went on drawing the cheques because I wanted a little change of air and scene now and then. You have no idea how it picked me up!"

"I saw in what society it set you down, Peter," was Sophia's chilling answer.

"You—you musn't think she is *always* like that," he urged. "It took me quite by surprise—it was a most painful position for me. I think, Sophia, your own sense of fairness will acknowledge that, considering the awkwardness of my situation, I—I behaved as well as could be expected. You do admit that, don't you?"

Sophia was silent for a minute or so before she spoke again.

"I must have time to think, Peter," she said: "it is all so strange, so contrary to all my experience, that I can hardly see things as yet in their proper light. But I may tell you at once that, from what I was able to observe, and from all you have just told me, I am inclined to think that you are free from actual culpability in the matter. It was quite clear that that very forward girl was the principal throughout, and that you were nothing more than an unwilling and most embarrassed accessory."

This was so much more lenient a view than he had dared to expect that Peter recovered his ordinary equanimity.

"That was all," he said. "I am very glad you saw it, my dear. I was perfectly helpless!"

"And then," said Sophia, "I was more than pleased by your firm refusal to commit suicide. What you said was so very sound and true, Peter."

"I hope so, said Peter, with much complacency. "Yes, I was pretty firm with her! By the way," he added, "you—you didn't happen to see whether she really did jump overboard, I suppose?"

"I came away just at the crisis," she said. "I thought you would tell *me!*"

"*I* came away, too," said Peter. "It doesn't matter, of course; but still I should have rather liked to know whether she meant it or not."

"How can you speak of it so heartlessly, Peter? She may have been trying to frighten you; she is just the kind of girl who would. But she may have been in earnest after all!"

"You see, Sophia," said Peter, "it doesn't matter whether she was or not—it isn't as if it had ever really happened."

"Not really happened? But I was *there*; I heard, I saw it—nothing could be more real!"

"At any rate," he said, "it only happens when I use those cheques; and she can't possibly carry out her rash intention until I draw another—which I promise you faithfully I will never do. If you doubt me, I will burn the book now before your eyes!"

With these words he went to the drawer and took out the cheque-book.

"No," said Sophia, "you must not do that, Peter. There is much about this Time Bank that I don't pretend to understand, that I can not account for by any known natural law; but I may not disbelieve my own eyes and ears! These events that have happened in the extra time you chose to defer till now are just as real as any other events. You *have* made this girl's acquaintance; you have—I don't say through any fault of your own, but

still you *have*—caused her to transfer her
affections from the man she was engaged to,
and, being a creature of ill-regulated mind and
no strength of character, she has resolved to
put an end to her life rather than meet his
just indignation. She is now on the very
point of accomplishing this folly. Well, badly
as she has behaved, you can not possibly leave
the wretched girl there! You must go back
at once, restrain her by main force, and not
leave her until you have argued her into a
rational frame of mind."

Peter was by no means anxious to go back
at first.

"It's not at all necessary," he said ; "and
besides, I don't know if you're aware of it,
but with the way these cheques are worked,
it's ten chances to one against my hitting off
the right fifteen minutes! Still," he added,
with an afterthought, " I can *try*, of course, if
you insist upon it. I can take my chance
with another fifteen minutes, but that must be
the last. I am sick and tired of this *Boomerang* business, I am indeed !"

Shameful as it is to state, he had altered
his mind from a sudden recollection that he

would not mind seeing Miss Tyrrell for just once more. He had not drawn her for several weeks.

"No," said Sophia, thoughtfully; "I see your objection—fifteen minutes is not enough, unless you could be sure of getting the successors to the last. But I have an idea, Peter —if you draw out the whole balance of your time, you can't possibly help getting the right fifteen minutes somewhere or other. I think that's logical?"

"Oh, devilish logical!" muttered Peter to himself, who had reasons, which he could not divulge to her, for strongly disapproving of such a plan.

"The fact is, my dear," he said, "it—it's rather late this evening to go away for any time!"

"You forget," she said, "that, however long you are away, you will come back at exactly the same time you start. But you have some other reason, Peter—you had better tell me!"

"Well," he owned, "I might come across some one I'd rather not meet."

"You are thinking of the man that girl

said she had been engaged to—Alfred, wasn't it?"

Peter had forgotten Alfred for the moment; and besides, he was not likely to turn up till the *Boomerang* got to Plymouth, and he knew his extra hours stopped before that. Still, Alfred did very well as an excuse.

"Ah!" he said, "Alfred. You heard what she said about him? A violent character—with a revolver, Sophia!"

"But you told her you were not afraid of him. I felt so proud of you when you said it. And think, you may be able to bring them together—to heal the breach between them!"

"He's more likely to make a breach in me that won't heal!" said Peter.

"Still, as you said yourself, it isn't as if it was all actually existing. What does it matter, even if he should shoot you?"

"I don't see any advantage in exposing myself to any such unpleasant experiences, even if they are only temporary," he said.

"It is not a question of advantage, Peter," rejoined Sophia; "it is a simple duty, and I'm surprised that you don't see it as such. What-

ever the consequences of your conduct may
be, you can not evade them like this; you
have chosen to begin, and you must go on!
I am quite clear about that. Let me see"—
(here she took the cheque-book, and made
some rapid calculations from the counterfoils)
—"yes, you have two hours and three-quarters
at least still standing to your credit; and then
there's the compound interest. I will tear out
all these small cheques and burn them." Which
she did as she spoke. "And now, Peter, sit
down and fill up one of the blank ones at the
end for the whole amount."

"Do you know, Sophia," said Peter, "it
occurs to me that this is just one of those
matters which can only be satisfactorily arranged by—er—a woman's tact. Suppose I
make the cheque payable to *you* now—eh?"

"You mean, that you want me to go instead
of you?" she asked.

"Well," said Peter, "if it wouldn't be
bothering you, my dear, I think perhaps it
would be—"

"Don't say another word," she interrupted,
"or I shall begin to *despise* you, Peter! If I
thought you meant it seriously, I would go up-

stairs, put on my bonnet, and go back to mamma forever. I could not bear to be the wife of a coward!"

"Oh, I'll go!" said Peter, in much alarm. "I said what I did out of consideration, not cowardice. But wouldn't to-morrow do just as well, Sophia? It is late to turn out!"

"To-morrow will *not* do as well," she said: "fill up that cheque to-night or you will lose me forever!"

"There!" said Peter, as he scrawled off the cheque. "Are you satisfied *now*, Sophia?"

"I shall be when I see you present it."

"Er—yes," he said; "oh! I mean to present it—presently. I—I think I'll take a small glass of brandy before I go, my dear, to keep the cold out."

"As you will certainly be in a summer, if not tropical, temperature the next moment," she said, "I should advise you to take nothing of the kind."

"I say," he suggested, "suppose I find she has jumped overboard—what shall I do then?"

"Do! Can you possibly ask? You will jump after her, of course!"

"It's easy to say 'of course,'" he said;

"but I never *could* swim more than twenty strokes!"

"Swim those twenty then, and let come what will; you will be back all the sooner. But don't stand there talking about it, Peter—go!"

"I'm going," he said meekly. "You'll sit up for me, Sophia, if—if I'm late, won't you?"

"Don't be absurd!" she said. "You know perfectly well that, as I said before, you won't be away a second."

"It won't be a second for you," he said, "but it will be several hours for *me;* and goodness only knows what I may have to go through in the time! However," he added, with an attempt to be cheerful, "it may all pass off quite pleasantly—don't you think it may, Sophia?"

"How *can* I tell? You will only find out by going."

"I'm going, my dear—I'm going at once! . . . You'll give me just one kiss before I start, won't you?"

"I will give you no kiss till you come back and I hear what you have done," said Sophia.

"Very well," he retorted; "you may be
sorry you refused when it's too late! I may
never come back at all, for anything I can
tell!"

And, little as he knew it, he spoke with an
almost prophetic anticipation of what was to
come. Never again was he destined to stand
on that hearth-rug!

But he dared not linger longer, as he could
see from her expression that she would suffer
no further trifling; and he slipped his last
cheque under the clock,—with consequences
that must be reserved for the next chapter.

10

CHAPTER VIII.

PAID IN HIS OWN COIN.

*In Suspense: a Gleam of Comfort.—Darkness Returns.
—The Rock Ahead.—Sir William Lends His Binocular.—Reappearance of an Old Enemy.—A New Danger.—Out of the Frying-pan.*

PETER found himself below this time, in the broad passage, furnished with seats and tables for writing, and which divided the passengers' cabins. Above, he heard a confused stir and bustle of excitement, the trampling of feet, the creaking and rattle of chains, orders shouted in English and Hindustani. From the absence of all vibration, in the vessel, it was evident that she had been brought to. *Why?*

Peter guessed the cause only too easily: the unhappy Miss Davenport had indeed succeeded in carrying out her rash design. She

had jumped overboard, and the captain had
stopped the engines and lowered a boat in the
hope of picking her up before she sank! And
he himself—why was he skulking below like
this? He had only too much reason to fear
that he must have been a witness of the fatal
leap; and, instead of plunging overboard to the
rescue as a hero ought, had rushed down here
ignominiously.

Had he been observed? Was his connec-
tion with the tragedy suspected? Could he
venture up on deck and inform himself? He
tried, but his nerve failed him, and he sank
into one of the chairs in a state of almost un-
bearable suspense.

Just at this moment, he saw the skirts of a
muslin gown appear at the head of the broad
companion which led to the dining-saloon.
Some one, a girl evidently, was descending.
Presently, he saw her fully revealed—it was
Miss Tyrrell.

Perhaps he had never been so glad to see
her before. She was a friend, a dear friend
She, at least, would sympathize with him,
would understand that it was not his fault if
he had been too late to avert a catastrophe.

She was coming to him. Her eyes were friendly and pitiful as they sought his. She, at least, did not turn from him!

"How pale, how terribly pale you look!" she said. "You must nerve yourself to see her—it can not be long now!"

"Has she been brought on board yet?" he gasped. "Is—is there any hope?"

"We shall know very soon. It is possible you may find that all is at an end."

"Ah! you think so? But—but no one will say it was *my* fault, will they? I—I was ready to make any sacrifice—only somehow, when the moment comes, I am apt to lose my presence of mind."

"Yes, I know," she said feelingly; "you are not quite yourself yet, but I know you would make the sacrifice if your duty demanded it. But she may have taken advantage of your absence to free herself and you from all obligation, may she not?"

This suggestion comforted Peter.

"She *must* have done!" he said. "Yes, of course. I could not be expected to prevent it, if I wasn't there; and I wasn't, when it came to the point. But, Miss Tyrrell, do you think that it is really all over? She—she may come round after all!"

"She may—but of course, if it is true that she is engaged to another, she can have no possible claim on *you*."

What a sensible right-minded way this girl had of looking at things! thought Peter, not for the first time.

"Why, of course she can't!" he cried. "And it *is* true. She is engaged—to a fellow of the name of Alfred."

"You know that as a fact?" she exclaimed.

"I know it from her own lips, and I need not say that I should be the last person to wish to—er—upset so desirable an arrangement."

"Why—*why* didn't you tell me all this before?" she inquired.

"I—I didn't think it would interest you," he replied.

Here, to Peter's utter astonishment, she covered her face with her hands.

"Not interest me!" she murmured at last. "Oh, how could you—how *could* you keep this from me? Can't you see—can't you guess what a difference it has made in my feelings?"

It might be very dull of him, but he could
not perceive why the fact of Miss Davenport's
engagement to Alfred should affect Miss Tyrrell so strangely as this!

"I may call you 'Peter' now," she said.
"Oh, Peter, *how* happy you have made me!
Why did you keep silence so long? It was too
quixotic! Don't you understand even yet?"

"No," said Peter, blankly, "I'm afraid I
don't."

"Then, if you are really so diffident, I—I
must tell you that if you were to ask a certain
question once more, I might—I don't say I
should, but I might—meet it with a different
answer!"

"Good Heavens!" he ejaculated, involuntarily.

"But you must not ask me yet—not just yet.
I must have time to consider. I must tell papa
before I decide anything. You *will* wait a
little longer, won't you, Peter?"

"Yes," he said, feeling limp, "I'll wait. I'd
rather!"

She smiled radiantly upon him, and then fled
lightly up the companion, leaving him with
fresh cause for uneasiness. He could no longer

doubt that, for some reason, she expected him
to propose to her, which it seemed he had already, in one of those confounded extra minutes, been unprincipled enough to do! Now
she had gone to inform her father, the judge,
and he would have the disagreeable task of
disabusing them before long!

At this point he started, believing that he
was visited by an apparition; for a cabin-door
opened, and Miss Davenport came out and
stood before him.

But she was so obviously flesh and blood
—and so dry—that he soon saw that all
his anxiety on her account had been superfluous.

"Then you—you didn't jump overboard
after all?" he faltered, divided between relief
and annoyance at having been made to come
back, as it were, on false pretenses.

"You know who prevented me, and by what
arguments!" she said, in a low strained voice.

"*Do* I?" he said, helplessly.

"Who should, if you do not? Did not you
implore me not to leave you, and declare that,
if I would only have courage and wait, we
should be happy even yet? And I *did* wait.

For what, I ask you, Peter Tourmalin—for *what?*"

"It's really no use asking *me*," he said, "for I've no idea!"

"I waited—to discover that all this time you have had a secret understanding with another; that you are about to transfer your fickle affections to—to that fair girl! Don't deny it, Peter! I was listening. I see it all—all!"

"I wish to goodness *I* did!" he said. "I never was in such a muddle as this in my life. I can only assure you that if that young lady really imagines that I am, or can be, anything more to her than a friend, she is entirely mistaken. I was just about to go up and explain as much to her father!"

"You are not deceiving me?" she asked, earnestly. "You are *sure?*"

"I will swear it, if you wish!" he replied.

"No," she said, relenting visibly, "your word is enough. I do believe you, and I am almost happy again. So long as you do not desert me, even Alfred loses half his terrors!"

"Exactly," he said; "and now, if you will excuse me, I'll just run up on deck and settle this other business."

He went up to the hurricane-deck, and found the ship had anchored. In front was a huge barren rock, with lines of forts, walls, and telegraph poles ; and at its base a small white town huddled. They had arrived at Gibraltar, which accounted for the absence of motion.

As he stood there, taking this in, he was accosted by Sir William Tyrrell, who thrust his arm through Peter's in a friendly manner.

" My dear boy," said the judge, heartily, " Violet has just told me the good news. I can only say that I am delighted—most delighted ! I have always felt a warm interest in you, ever since that affair of—"

" Of the monkey," said Peter. " I am very glad to hear it, Sir William ; but—but I ought to tell you that I am afraid Miss Tyrrell was —a little premature. She misinterpreted a remark of mine, which, in point of fact, referred to somebody else altogether."

" Then you have no more reason than before for assuming that your *fiancée* has thrown you over. Am I to understand that ? "

" No more reason than before," admitted Peter.

" And your uncertainty still continues ? Very

unsatisfactory, I must say! I do think, my dear
fellow, that, in your position, you should have
been more careful to refrain from betraying any
interest in Violet until you knew that you were
free to speak. As it is, you may have cast a
shadow upon her young life that it may take
years to dispel!"

Peter's heart sank into his boots for very
shame at this gentle and almost paternal re-
proof.

"Yes," continued the worthy judge, "Violet is a high-minded girl, scrupulously sensitive
on points of honor; and, unless the young lady
you are under a semi-engagement to should release you of her own free will, I know my daughter too well to doubt that she will counsel you
to fulfill your contract and renounce all hope
so far as she is concerned."

Peter felt a little easier.

"I—I am prepared to do that," he said.

"Well, I don't say myself that I go quite so
far as she does; but strictly, no doubt, a promise is a promise, and should be kept at all hazards. You have done all that a man can hon-
orably do to put himself right. You have
written to this young lady, so I understand,

informing her of the change in your sentiments, and offering, nevertheless, to redeem
your promise if she insisted upon it. I think
that was the general purport of your letter."

Here was one more evil fruit of his extra
time! What would Sophia think, or say, or
do, if such a letter as that ever came to her
knowledge? Fortunately, that at least was
impossible!

"You have some grounds," the judge went
on, "for assuming that the lady has already
treated the contract as non-existent—a person
called Alfred, I think my daughter said?"

"No, that was a mistake," explained Peter.
"Alfred is engaged to quite a different person."

"Well, in any case, it is quite possible that
you may obtain your release when you meet
her; and your suspense will soon be over now.
Miss—er—Pincher, is it?—will probably be
on board the ship before many minutes. I
see the boats are putting out from the harbor
already."

"*What!*" cried Peter, with the terrible conviction darting through his mind that Sir William spoke the bare truth.

Sophia had said something about meeting

him at Gibraltar; but if she had done so during the real voyage, how could he have the
meeting all over again, with this ghastly vari-
ation? If he could only remember whether
she had come out, or not! It was singular,
incomprehensible! But his memory was a
blank on such a vital fact as this!

"Would you like to have my field-glass for a
moment?" said Sir William, considerately.

Peter took them, and the next moment the
binocular fell from his nerveless hands. He
had seen only too clearly the familiar form of
Sophia seated in the peaked stern of a small
craft which a Spanish boatman was "scissoring"
through the waves toward the *Boomerang*.

"Come, courage!" said the Judge kindly,
as he picked up his glass and wiped the lenses.
"Don't be nervous, my boy. You don't know
what she may have to say to you yet, you know!"

"No, I don't!" he groaned. "I—I think
I ought to go down to the gangway and meet
her," he added, tremulously—not that he had
any intention of doing so, but he wanted to be
alone.

Before the Judge could even express his
approbation of Peter's course, Tourmalin was

down on the saloon-deck seeking a quiet spot wherein to collect his thoughts.

Before he could find the quiet spot, however, he almost ran into the arms of the matron from Melbourne, whom he had not seen since the episode of the music-room.

"A word with you, Mr. Tourmalin!" she said.

"I—I really can't stop now," stammered Peter. "I—I'm expecting friends!"

"I, too," she said, "am expecting a relation, and it is for that reason that I wish to speak to you now. My brother, who has been staying at Gibraltar on account of his health, will be as determined as I am to trace and punish the infamous calumny upon the name and career of our honored parent."

"I dare say, madam," said Peter—"I dare say. Very creditable to you both—but I really can't stop just now!"

"You appear to forget, sir, that, unless you can satisfactorily establish your innocence, my brother will certainly treat you as the person primarily responsible for an atrocious slander!"

"A slander—upon your father! . . . *Me?*"

said the indignant Peter. "Why, I never
heard of the gentleman!"

"Denial will not serve you now," she said.
"I have not only your own admissions in the
music-room, but the evidence of more than
one trustworthy witness, to prove that you
circulated a report that my dear father—one
of the most honored and respected citizens of
Melbourne—began his Colonial career as—as
a transported convict!"

After all, as the hapless Peter instantly saw,
he *might* have said so, for anything he knew,
in one of those still unexhausted extra quarters
of an hour!

"If I said so, I was misinformed," he
said.

"Just so; and in our conversation on the
subject, you mentioned the name of the person who used you as his mouthpiece to dis-
seminate his malicious venom. What I wish
to know now is, whether you are prepared or
not to repeat that statement?"

Peter recollected now that he had used ex-
pressions implicating Mr. Perkins although
merely as the origin of totally different complications.

"I can't positively go so far as that," he said. "I—I made the statement generally."

"As you please," she said. "I can merely say that my brother, whom I expect momentarily, is, although an invalid in some respects, a powerful and determined man; and unless you repeat in his presence the sole excuse you have to offer, he will certainly horsewhip you in the presence of the other passengers. That is all, sir!"

"Thank you—it's quite enough!" murmured Peter, thinking that Alfred himself could hardly be much more formidable; and he slipped down the companion to the cabin-saloon, where he found Miss Davenport anxiously expecting him.

"He is here," she whispered. "I have just seen him through the port-hole."

"What—the old lady's brother!" he replied.

"He has *no* sister who is an old lady. I mean Alfred."

"*Alfred?*" he almost yelped. "Alfred *here!*"

"Of course he is here. Is not his battalion stationed at Gibraltar? You knew it, we were to meet him here!"

"I didn't, indeed—or I should never have come!" he protested.

"Don't let us waste words now. He is here; he will demand an explanation from you. He has his pistol with him—I could tell by the bulge under his coat. We must both face him; and the question is, What are you going to say?"

Peter thrust his hands through his carefully parted hair:

"Say!" he repeated. "I shall tell him the simple, straightforward truth. I shall frankly admit that we have walked, and sat, and talked together; but I shall assure him, as I can honestly, that during the whole course of our acquaintance I have never once regarded you in any other light but that of a friend."

"And you suppose that, knowing how I have changed, he will believe that!" she cried. "He will fire long before you can finish one of those fine sentences!"

"In that case," suggested Peter, "why tell him anything at all? Why not spare him, poor fellow, at all events for the time? It will only upset him just now. Let him suppose that we are strangers to one another; and

you can break the truth to him gently when
you reach England, you know. I'm sure that's
much the more sensible plan!"

She broke into strange mirthless laughter.

"Your prudence comes too late," she said.
"You forget that the truth was broken to him
some days ago, in the letter I wrote from Brin-
disi."

"You wrote and broke it to him at Brin-
disi!" cried Peter. "What induced you to do
that?"

"Why, *you!*" she retorted. "You insisted
that it was due to him; and though I knew
better than you what the effect would be, I
dared not tell you the whole truth. I wanted
to end the engagement, too; and I scarcely
cared then what consequences might follow.
Now they are upon us, and it is useless to try
to escape them. Since we *must* die, let us go
up on deck and get it over!"

"One moment," he said; "Alfred can wait
a little. I—I must go to my cabin first, and
put on a clean collar."

And with this rather flimsy pretext, he
again made his escape. He made up his mind
what to do as he rushed toward his cabin. He

11

could hardly have been anything like an hour on board the *Boomerang* as yet; he had to get through at least another three before he could hope for deliverance. His only chance was to barricade himself inside his cabin, and stead-fastly refuse to come out, upon any considera-tion whatever, until he was released by the natural expiration of time.

He sped down the passage, and found, to his horror, that he had forgotten the number of his berth. However, he knew where it ought to be, and darted into an open door, which he fastened securely with hook and bolt, and sank breathless on one of the lower berths.

"You seem in a hurry, my friend!" said a voice opposite; and Peter's eyes, unused at first to the comparative dimness, perceived that a big man was sitting on the opposite berth, engaged in putting on a pair of spiked cricket-shoes. He had bolted himself inside the cabin with Mr. Perkins!

CHAPTER IX.

COMPOUND INTEREST.

*Back to the Fire Again.—A Magnanimous Return.—
Catching at Straws.—Two Total Strangers.—Purely
a Question of Precedence.—"Hemmed in" and "Sur-
rounded."—The Last Chance.*

THE Bank Manager looked across at Peter
with an amused smile; he seemed quite friendly. Whether he was in Peter's cabin, or Peter
in his, did not appear; and perhaps it was
not of much consequence either way. If the
cabin belonged to Mr. Perkins, he did not, at
all events, appear to resent the intrusion.

"You seem rather put out about something,"
he said again, as Peter was still too short of
breath for words.

"Oh, no," panted Peter, "it's nothing.
There was so much bustle going on above that
I thought I'd come in here for a little quiet;
that's all."

"Well," said the manager, "I'm glad you looked in; for, as it happens, you're the very man I wanted to see. I dare say you're wondering why I'm putting on these things?"

Peter nodded his head, which was all he felt equal to.

"Why, I've just been having a talk with that old she-griffin from Melbourne. Perhaps you don't know that her brother is coming on board directly?"

"O yes, I *do?*" said Peter.

"Well, it seems she means to denounce me to him as the slanderer of her father. She may, if she chooses; my conscience is perfectly clear on that score. No one can bring anything of the sort home to me; and I've no doubt I shall soon satisfy him that I'm as innocent as an unborn babe. Still, I want you, as a respectable man and the only real friend I have on board, to come with me and be my witness that you never heard such a rumor from my lips; and besides, sir, we shall have an opportunity at last of seeing the unutterable scamp who has had the barefaced impudence to say I told him this precious story! She's going to produce him, sir; and if he dares to

stand me out to my face—well, *he*'ll know why
I've put on these shoes! Come along; I can't
let you off."

Peter dared not refuse, for fear of attracting
his friend's suspicions. He could only trust
to slipping away in the confusion ; and so, un-
fastening the cabin-door, the manager caught
the unresisting Tourmalin tightly by the arm,
and hurried him along the central passage and
up the companion.

Even Miss Davenport would have been a
welcome diversion at that moment; but she
was not there to intercept him, and he reached
the upper deck more dead than alive.

" Where's that old vixen *now?* " exclaimed
the Manager, dropping Peter's arm. " Here,
just stay where you are a minute, till I find her
and her confounded brother!"

He bustled off, leaving Tourmalin by the
davits, quite incapable of action of any kind in
the presence of this new and awful dilemma.
He had been spreading a cruel and unjustifia-
ble slander against an irreproachable colonial
magnate, whose son was now at hand to demand reparation with a horsewhip. He could
only propitiate him by denouncing Perkins as

his informant, and if he did that he would be kicked from one end of the ship to the other with a spiked boot! This was Nemesis indeed, and it was Sophia who had insisted upon his exposing himself to it. What a fool he was not to fly back to that cabin while he could!

He turned to flee, and as he did so a hand was passed softly through his arm.

"Not *that* way, Peter!" said Miss Tyrrell's voice.

A wild, faint hope came to him that he might be going to receive one of the back quarters of an hour. The caprices of the Time Cheques were such that it was quite possible he would be thrown back into an earlier interview. Little as he felt inclined for any social intercourse just then, he felt that it would afford him a brief interlude—would at least give him breathing-time before his troubles began again.

"I will go wherever you choose," he said; "I am in your hands."

"I came," she said, "to take you to her. She is asking for you."

"She?" said Peter. "For heaven's sake, *who*?"

"Why, Miss Pinceney, of course. I knew who it was directly I saw her face. Peter, is it true, as papa tells me, that I misunderstood you just now—that she is *not* engaged to Alfred?"

"Alfred? No!" he replied. "If she is engaged to any one at all, I have strong grounds for supposing it's to me!"

"Then we must submit, that is all," said Miss Tyrrell. "But we do not know her decision yet; there is still hope!"

"Yes," he said, "there is hope still. Let us go to her; make haste!"

He meant what he said. Sophia could at least extricate him from a portion of his difficulties. Miss Tyrrell—magnanimous and unselfish girl that she was, in spite of her talent for misapprehension—was ready to resign him to a prior claim, if one was made. And Sophia was bound to claim him; for if the engagement between them had been broken off, he could not now be her husband, as he was. Even Time Cheques must recognize accomplished facts.

He followed her across the ship, turning down the very passage in which he had sat

through more than one cheque with Miss
Davenport; and on the opposite side he found
Sophia standing, with her usual composure,
waiting for his arrival.

She was so identically the same Sophia that
he had left so lately, that he felt reassured.
She, at least, could not be the dupe of all this.
She had come—how, he did not trouble himself to think,—but she had come with the
benevolent intention of saving him !

" How do you do, my love ?" he began. " I
—I thought I should see you here."

" You only see me here, Peter," she replied,
in a voice that trembled slightly, in spite of
her efforts to command it, " because I felt
very strongly that it was my duty to put an end
at the earliest moment to a situation which has
become impossible ! "

" I'm sure," said Peter, " it is quite time it
was put an end to—it couldn't go on like this
much longer."

" It shall not, if I can help it," she said.
" Miss Tyrrell, pray don't go away; what I
have to say concerns you too."

" No ; don't go away, Miss Tyrrell," added
Peter, who felt the most perfect confidence in

Sophia's superior wisdom, and was now persuaded that somehow it was all going to be explained. "Sir William, will you kindly step this way too? Sir William Tyrrell—Miss Pinceney. Miss Pinceney has something to tell you which will make my position thoroughly clear."

"I have only to say," she said, "that your honorable and straightforward conduct, Peter, has touched me to the very heart. I feel that I am the only person to blame, for it was I who insisted upon you subjecting yourself to this test."

"It was," said Peter. "I told you something would happen—and it has!"

"I would never hold you to a union from which all love on your side had fled; do not think so, Peter. And now that I see my—my rival, I confess that I could expect no other result. So, dear Miss Tyrrell, I resign him to you freely—yes, cheerfully—for, by your womanly self-abnegation you have proved yourself the worthier. Take her, Peter; you have my full consent!"

"My dear young lady," said the Judge, deeply affected, "this is most noble of you! Allow me to shake you by the hand."

"I can't thank you, dear, *dear*, Miss Pin-ceney!" sobbed his daughter. "Peter, tell her for me how we shall both bless and love her all our lives for this!"

Peter's brain reeled. Was *this* Sophia's notion of getting him out of a difficulty?

As he gazed distractedly around, his eyes became fixed and glazed with a new terror. A stalwart stranger, with a bushy red beard, was coming toward him, with a stout riding-whip in his right hand. By his side walked the Manager, from whose face all vestige of friend-liness had vanished.

"As soon as you have quite finished your conversation with these ladies," said the Man-ager, with iron politeness, "this gentleman would be glad of a few moments with you; after which I shall request your attention to a little personal affair of my own. Don't let us *hurry* you, you know!"

"I—I won't," returned Peter, flurriedly; "but I'm rather busy just now: a little later, I—I shall be delighted."

As he stood there, he was aware that they had withdrawn to a bench some distance away, where they conferred with the elderly lady from Melbourne. He could feel their angry glare upon him, and it contributed to rob him of the little self-possession he had left.

"Sophia," he faltered piteously, "I say this is too bad—it is, really! You *can't* mean to leave me in such a hole as this—do let's get home at once!"

Before she could make any reply to an appeal which seemed to astonish her considerably, a thin, bilious-looking man, with a face twitching with nervous excitement, a heavy black mustache, and haggard eyes, in which a red fire smoldered, appeared at the gangway and joined the group.

"I beg your pardon," he said, lifting his hat; "forgive me if I interrupt you, but my business is urgent—most urgent! Perhaps you could kindly inform me if there is a—a gentleman" (the word cost him a manifest struggle to pronounce)—"a gentleman on board of the name of Tourmalin? I have a little matter of business" (here his right hand stole to his breast-pocket) "to transact with him," he explained, with a sinister smile that caused Peter to give suddenly at the knees.

"It's that infernal Alfred!" he thought. "Now I *am* done for!"

"Why," said Miss Tyrrell, who was clinging affectionately to Peter's arm, "*this* is Mr. Tourmalin! You can speak to him now—here, if you choose. We have no secrets from one another—have we, Peter?"

"I have lately learned," said the gloomy man, "that a certain Mr. Tourmalin has stolen from me the affection of one who was all heaven and earth to me!"

"Then it *must* be another Mr. Tourmalin," said Miss Tyrrell, "not this one; because—surely you do not need to be told that you have no rivalry to fear from him?" she broke off, with a blush of charming embarrassment.

Alfred's scowl distinctly relaxed, and Peter felt that, after all, this unfortunate misunderstanding on Miss Tyrrell's part might prove serviceable to him. Since Sophia, for reasons of her own, refused to assist him, he must accept any other help that offered itself.

"The best proof I can give you of my innocence," he said, "is to mention that I have the honor to be engaged to this lady."

He heard a stifled shriek from behind him

as he made this assertion, and the next moment Miss Davenport, who must have come up in time to catch the last words, had burst into the center of the group.

"It is not true!" she cried. "Alfred, you must not believe him!"

"Not *true?*" exclaimed Alfred, Sophia, Miss Tyrrell, and Sir William, in the same breath.

"No!" said Miss Davenport; "at least, if he has really engaged himself, it is within the last few minutes, and with the chivalrous intention of shielding *me!* Peter, I will not be shielded by such means. Our love is too precious to be publicly denied. I can not suffer it; I will acknowledge it, though it costs me my life! You," she added, turning to Sophia —"you can prove that I speak the truth. It was to you that I confided, that day we met on deck, the story of our fatal attachment."

"I really think you must be mistaken," said Sophia coldly. "If you confided such a story to anybody, it could not have been to me; for, until a few minutes ago, I had never set foot upon this ship."

How Sophia could stand there and, remembering, as she must do, her recent appropri-

ation of the Time Cheque, tell such a down-
right fib as this, passed Peter's comprehension.
But, as her statement was in his favor so far
as it went, he knew better than to contradict
it.

"Whether it was you or not," insisted Miss
Davenport, "it is he and no one else who
rendered my engagement to Alfred utterly
repugnant to me! Can you look at him now,
and doubt me longer?"

"So, Peter," said Sophia severely, "you
could not even be faithful to your unfaithful-
ness!"

Miss Tyrrell made no comment, but she
dropped his arm as if it had scorched her
fingers, whereupon Miss Davenport clung to it
in her stead, to Peter's infinite dismay and confusion.

"He *is* faithful!" she cried. "It is only
a mistaken sense of honor that made him apparently false. Yes, Alfred, what I wrote to
you, and the postscript he added, is the simple truth. We can not command our own
hearts. Such love as I once had for you is
dead—it died on the fatal day which brought
him across my path. We met—we love; deal

with us as you will ! I would rather, ever so
much rather, die with him than lose him
now ! ”

Alfred was already beginning to fumble
fiercely in his breast-pocket. Peter felt the
time had arrived for plain speaking ; he could
not submit to be butchered under a ridiculous
misapprehension of this kind.

“ Listen to me ! ” he said eagerly, “ before
you do anything rash, or you may bitterly regret it afterward. I do assure you that I am
the victim—we are all the victims of a series
of unfortunate cheques—I should say, mis-
takes. It's absurd to make me responsible for
the irregular proceedings of a nonsensical
Bank. If I had spent my time as I ought to
have done at the time, instead of putting it
out on deposit I should never have dreamed
of employing it in any kind of philandering ! ”

“ That,” said Sophia, “ is undeniable ; but
you spent it as you ought not to have done ! ”

“ Such a speech comes ill from you,” he
said, reproachfully, “ after having expressly
condoned the past ; and, however I may have
appeared to philander, I can conscientiously

declare that my sentiments toward both of these young ladies—*both*, you understand— have been restricted to a respectful and—and merely friendly esteem. . . . Don't shoot, Alfred ! . . . I thought that was quite understood on all sides. Only have a little more patience, Alfred, and I will undertake to convince even you that I could not for a moment have contemplated depriving you of the hand of this extremely charming and attractive lady, who will *not* let go my arm. . . . I—I am a married man ! "

" Married ! " shrieked Miss Davenport, cowering back.

" Married ! " exclaimed Miss Tyrrell, as she hid her face upon her father's shoulder.

" Maried ! " shouted the Judge. " By heavens, sir, you shall account to me for this ! "

" Married ! " cried Sophia.. " Oh, Peter, I was *not* prepared for this ! When ? Where ? "

" *When ? Where ?* " he echoed. " You were not prepared for it ? Perhaps you will ask me next who my wife is ! "

" I shall not indeed," said Sophia, " for I have no longer the slightest curiosity on such a subject ! "

Peter collapsed upon the nearest bench.

"Sophia?" he cried hoarsely, "why keep this up any longer? Surely it is gone far enough—you *can't* pretend you don't know!"

But while he spoke the words, he saw suddenly that his attempt to force her hand was hopeless: she was quite sincere in her surprise; she was the Sophia of *six months ago*, and no amount of explanation could ever make her comprehend what had happened since that time!

And here Alfred broke his silence.

"What you have just confessed," he said, "removes my last scruple. I might, for all I can tell, have stayed my hand and spared your life upon your promise to make Maud happy; for, in spite of her treatment of me, her happiness is still my first consideration. But now you have declared that impossible,—why, as soon as I can get this revolver out of my pocket—for it has stuck in the confounded lining—I will shoot you like a rabbit!"

"Sir William," cried Peter, "I appeal to you! You are the representative of Law and Order here. He is threatening a breach of the Peace—the *Queen's* Peace! I call upon you to interfere!"

12

"I am no advocate," said Sir William, with judicial calm, "for taking the law into one's own hands. I even express a hope that this gentleman will not carry out his avowed intention, at least until I have had time to withdraw, and I must not be understood to approve his action in any way. At the same time, I am distinctly of opinion that he has received sufficient provocation to excuse even such extreme measures, and that the fate he threatens will, if summary, at least be richly deserved."

"I think so too," said Sophia, "though it would be painful to be compelled to witness it!"

"Terrible!" agreed Miss Tyrrell. "Let us hide our eyes, dear!"

"Stay, Alfred!" Miss Davenport implored, "have some pity! Think — with all your faults, you are a keen sportsman—you would not shoot even a rabbit sitting! Give Mr. Tourmalin a start of a few seconds—let him have a run before you fire!"

All this time Alfred was still fumbling for and execrating the obstinate weapon.

"I decline to run!" Peter cried from his seat; he knew too well that he could not stir a limb. "Shoot me sitting, or not at all, but don't keep me waiting any longer!"

His prayer seemed likely to be granted, for Alfred had at last succeeded in extricating the revolver; but before he could take aim, the Bank Manager and the Melbourne man ran in and interposed.

"Hold on one minute, sir," they said; "we, too, have business with the gentleman on the seat there, and you will admit that it must be concluded before yours, if it is to be settled at all. We must really ask you to postpone your little affair until we have finished. We will not keep you waiting any longer than we can help."

The Judge, with an ostentatious indifference, had strolled away to the smoking-room, probably to avoid being called upon to decide so nice a point as this disputed precedence; his daughter, Miss Davenport, and Sophia, had turned their backs, and, stopping their ears, were begging to be told when all was over.

Alfred was struggling to free his pistol-arm, which was firmly held by the other two men, and all three were talking at once in hot and

argumentative support of their claims. As
for Peter, he sat and looked on, glued to his
seat by terror: if he had any preference among
the disputants, he rather hoped that Alfred
would be the person to gain his point.

All at once he saw Sophia turn round and,
with her fingers still pressed to her ears, make
energetic contortions of her lips, evidently for
his benefit. After one or two repetitions, he
made out the words she was voicelessly fram-
ing.

"*Run for it!*" he interpreted. "*Quick
. . . while you can!*"

With his habitual respect for her advice, he
rose and, finding that the power of motion had
suddenly returned, he *did* run for it; he
slipped quietly round the corner and down the
passage to the other side of the ship, where he
hoped to reach the saloon-entrance, and eventually regain his cabin.

Unhappily for him, the grim lady from Melbourne had noted his flight and anticipated its
object. Long before he got to the open doors,
he saw her step out and bar the way; she had
an open sunshade in her hand, which she was
preparing to use as a butterfly net.

He turned and fled abruptly in the opposite
direction, intending to cross the bridge which
led aft to the second-class saloon deck, where
he might find cover; but as he saw, on turning
the corner, the Manager had already occupied
the passage, Peter turned again and doubled
back across the ship, making for the forecastle;
but he was too late, for the Melbourne man
was there before him, and cut off all hope of
retreat in that quarter.

There was only one thing left now; he must
take to the rigging, and accordingly the next
moment, scarcely knowing how he came there,
he was clambering up the shrouds for dear
life!

Higher and higher he climbed, slipping and
stumbling, and catching his unaccustomed feet
in the ratlins at every step; and all the way he
had a dismal conviction that as yet he had not
nearly exhausted the check he had drawn. He
must have at least another couple of hours to
get through, not to mention the compound interest, which the bank seemed characteristically
enough to be paying first.

Still, if he could only stay quietly up aloft
till his time was up, he might escape the worst

yet. Surely it was a sufficient penalty for his folly to have embroiled himself with every creature he knew; to have been chivied about the deck of an ocean steamer by three violent men, each thirsting for his blood; and to be reduced to mount the rigging like an escaped monkey!

A few more steps and he was safe at last! Just above was a huge yard, flattened on the upper surface, with a partially furled sail, behind which he could crouch unseen; his hands were almost upon it, when a bronzed and bearded face appeared above the canvas—it was one of the English crew.

"Beg your pardon, sir," said the man, civilly enough, "but I shall 'ave fur to trouble you to go down agin, please. Capt'in's strick orders, sir. Passengers ain't allowed to amuse theirselves climbing the rigging!"

"My good man!" said Peter, between his pants, "do I *look* as if I was amusing myself? I am pursued, I tell you. As an honest, good-hearted British seaman—which I am sure you are—I entreat you to give me a hand up, and hide me; it—it may be life or death for me!"

The man wavered; the desperate plight Peter was in seemed to arouse his compassion, as it well might.

"I *could* 'ide yer, I suppose, come to that," he said slowly; "but it's too late to think o' that now. Look below, sir!"

Peter glanced down between his feet, and saw two swarthy Lascars climbing the rigging like cats. Lower still, he had a bird's-eye view of the deck, about which his enemies were posted in readiness for his arrival: the Manager exhibiting his spiked boots to Sir William, who shook his head in mild deprecation; the old lady shaking her sunshade in angry denunciation, while her brother flourished his horsewhip; and Alfred stood covering him with his revolver, prepared to pick him off the instant he came within range!

And Peter hung there by his hands—for his feet had slipped out of the ratlins—as helpless a target as any innocent bottle in a shooting-gallery, and the Lascars were getting nearer and nearer!

He could see their bilious eyeballs, and their teeth gleaming in their dusky faces. He felt a bony hand reaching for his ankles, and then a dizziness came over him; his grip upon the coarse, tarry cordage relaxed, and, shutting his eyes, he fell—down—down—down. Would the fall never come to an end? Would he never arrive? . . .

CHAPTER X.

DÉNOUEMENT.

At last! The shock was over; and he feebly opened his eyes once more, to find that he was undoubtedly on the deck; and, yes, the Bank Manager was standing over him with a kind of triumphant grin!

"Mercy!" Peter murmured faintly. "You—you surely wouldn't kick a man when he's down!"

"My dear sir!" protested the Manager, "why should I wish to kick you in *any* position?"

He must be fatally injured, if even the Manager had relented!

"Is—is Alfred there?" asked Tourmalin, anxiously. "Keep him away, if you can!"

"Certainly!" said Mr. Perkins. "Who *is* Alfred?"

" Why, the—man with the revolver.   I
thought you knew ! "

" Come, come," said the Manager, " there's
no man of that kind here, I assure you.   Pull
yourself together, sir ; you're on board the
Boomerang now ! "

" I know," said Peter, dolefully,—" I know
I am ! "

He shut his eyes resignedly.   He was about
to receive some other portion of his time-bal-
ance.   If he could only hope that no fresh
complications would arise !   Would he meet
Miss Tyrrell or Miss Davenport next, he wondered, and how would they behave ?

" Haven't you had sleep enough yet ? " said
the Manager.   " You're not more than half-
awake even now ! "

" Sleep ? " exclaimed Tourmalin, sitting up
and rubbing his eyes.   " Why, you don't mean
to tell me I've been dreaming all this time ? "

" I don't know about dreaming ; but I can
answer for your snoring.   Why, you almost
drowned the ship's band !   I knew what would
happen when you *would* have two helpings of
curry at breakfast.   Worst thing to take in the
world, especially if you don't walk it off !

Why, you've been the joke of the whole ship
for the last half-hour. I wish you could have
seen yourself, with your head hanging over
the arm of your chair and your mouth wide
open! I thought at last it was only kind to
wake you up. Those two young ladies over
there have been in fits of laughter!"

Peter picked up Buckle, which was lying
face downward on the deck. His own face
was very red, possibly from stooping, as he inquired:

"Er—*which* two young ladies?"

"Can't tell you their names; but those two
uncommonly nice-looking girls—one in white
and navy-blue, and the darker one in pink.
Dear me, I thought they would have died!"

Even now they seemed to have the greatest
difficulty in controlling their countenances, for
happening just then to look round and catch
Peter's glance of confused and still somnolent
suspicion, they buried their faces in their hand-
kerchiefs once more, in agonies of suppressed
mirth.

And these were the two whom his dreaming
fancies had pictured as tenderly, desperately,
madly devoted to him! The reality was de-

cidedly disenchanting: they were very ordinary girls, he saw, after all.

"Well," said Mr. Perkins, "it's not far off
tiffin time now; so, you see, you managed to
get through your extra time after all!"

"Yes," said Peter, with a little natural embarrassment; "but I think, do you know, that,
on reflection, I—I *won't* deposit the extra
hours after all! If you will kindly take back
the—the check-book," he added, feeling in his
pockets, "and give me the form I signed, we
will consider the arrangement canceled—eh?"

"It's my belief," said the Manager, "that
your head isn't quite clear yet; for, hang me
if I know what you're talking about! Deposit? check-book? form? What is it all
about?"

Peter colored more furiously than before.

"It was the curry," he said. "I wasn't
quite sure whether—but it's really too absurd
to explain. I am wide-awake now, at all
events!"

He was awake now, and knew that no time-
bargain of this monstrous kind had ever been
actually effected, and all the wild events which
seemed to have taken whole months to accom-

plish themselves, were the work of a single hour's indigestion! He was still a bachelor; still engaged to Sophia: he had still to make the acquaintance of Miss Tyrrell and Miss Davenport, and endure the ordeal of remaining for some weeks to come—to say nothing of the extra hours—exposed to the peril of their fascinations!

But whatever happened now, it could not be said, at least, that he had not received abundant warning of the consequences which might ensue from any yielding, however blameless or defensible, on his part.

And Peter Tourmalin resolved that henceforth Buckle should monopolize his attention.

THE EPILOGUE.

THERE are always a few inquiring persons who, at the conclusion of any story, insist upon being told " what happened after that." And if such a question is ever justified, it is so in the case of a narrative that, as in the present instance, ends almost at the precise moment at which it began.

So it is not impossible that some readers may be sufficiently interested to wish to know the particular effect produced upon Peter Tourmalin's subsequent conduct by a vision more than usually complicated and connected.

Did he receive it, for example, as a solemnly prophetic warning, and forswear all female society while on the *Boomerang?* or was he rather prompted to prove its fallibility by actual experience?

As to the motives which guided him, we are

unable to speak with confidence, and they must
be left to be accounted for by the reader's
knowledge of human nature in general, and
Peter's, so far as it has been self-revealed by
his unconscious imagination in these pages, in
particular.

But the author is in a position to state with
certainty that, when Sophia and her mother
met the ship, as they duly did at Gibraltar,
nothing on Peter's part gave them the slightest ground for suspecting that he was on terms
of even the most distant acquaintanceship with
either Miss Tyrrell or Miss Davenport, and
that the fact of his being far advanced in the
third volume of Buckle's *History of Civilization* seemed to guarantee that he had employed
his spare time on board the vessel both wisely
and well.

Nor did he get into any difficulties by circu-
lating gossip concerning any matron from Melbourne, owing to the circumstance that there
was no lady passenger who at all answered the
description. She, like much else in his experiences, was purely a creation of the curry.

Lastly, it may be added that Peter is now
married to his Sophia, and is far happier than

even he could have expected. She tempers her intellectuality out of consideration for his mental barrenness; and as yet he has never found her society in the least oppressive, nor has his errant fancy wandered back in any perfidious sense to the time he spent, when freed from her supervision, on board the *Boomerang*.

THE END.

www.ingramcontent.com/pod-product-compliance
Lightning Source LLC
Chambersburg PA
CBHW030557040726
47497CB00008B/2767